THE BODY ON THE BEACH

Jane Austen Investigations
Book Three

Laura Martin

SAPERE
BOOKS

THE BODY ON
THE BEACH

Published by Sapere Books.

24 Trafalgar Road, Ilkley, LS29 8HH

saperebooks.com

ISBN: 978-0-85495-203-8

CHAPTER ONE

Lyme Regis, July 1798

The air was crisp and cool as Jane Austen wound her way up
the coastal path. The oppressive heat of the previous day had
given her an awful headache, so she was pleased to be out
walking this morning. It was still early, well before seven, and
she had crept out of the room she shared with Cassandra in
their holiday lodgings, leaving her sister sleeping.

The path was steep in places, set back a little from the cliff
edge for the first part of the climb. It was worth the effort,
however, for further along were glorious views over the bay
and out to sea. This was Jane's favourite thing about Lyme
Regis. Whereas Cassandra enjoyed the orderly beauty of the
promenade and strolling along the stone harbour wall —
known as the Cobb — Jane preferred the wild vistas afforded
from the cliffs.

A few days earlier, when they had first arrived in Lyme Regis,
Jane had persuaded Cassandra to walk the two miles along the
cliffs to Charmouth after lunch. There had been a few other
people on the coastal path, enjoying the sunshine and the
views, a mix of locals and visitors to the seaside towns. Now,
at this early hour, there was no one else in sight. As Jane
paused to look out over the shimmering sea, she felt a
wonderful peace spread through her. In her mind there was
nothing more beautiful than the rolling countryside that
surrounded her home in Hampshire, but the prettiness of the
coast here in the south of England came a very close second.
There was something enchanting about the long stretches of

sand backed by the multi-coloured cliffs, the hills rising gently behind.

Jane continued climbing until she was at the top of the cliff. The path wound in and out and in some places it clung to the very edge of the cliffs, some of the path having fallen away to the beach below.

Stopping to catch her breath, Jane held her bonnet to her head and looked out to sea. She strained her eyes, wondering if one day she might catch a glimpse of France only a short distance across the water. Her eyes wandered to the waves below as they lapped gently at the sand, swallowing up the beach and then spitting it back out with each new surge of water.

The tide must have turned a few hours earlier, for now it was slowly inching towards the cliffs. Jane's gaze followed it in and then she stiffened as she saw something out of the ordinary on the beach. A few feet from the base of the cliffs, a little further along towards Charmouth, was a body. At first she wondered if it was someone resting, enjoying the morning sunlight on the soft sand, but the longer she looked the more concerned she became. There was no movement whatsoever, not even the subtle shift the body makes when relaxing.

For a long moment Jane couldn't tear her eyes away, willing the person to move, to sit up or fling out an arm.

"Hello," she called down, raising her voice as loud as it would go. "Are you hurt?"

She looked along the cliffs towards Charmouth and then back down the coastal path to Lyme Regis, but there was no one around. The fisherman would have been up before dawn to take their boats out to the best fishing spots, and the visitors to Lyme Regis were not yet up to enjoy all the charms of the seaside town.

Jane peered over the cliff and then hastily took a step back. There was a sheer drop to jagged rocks, which in turn led haphazardly down to the sand. Even if she was sure-footed, it would be impossible to get down the cliffs quickly or safely. She would have to go round.

Without any further hesitation, Jane gathered her skirts and began to make her way back down the path she had climbed only a few minutes earlier. Despite her pace, it seemed to take an age to descend, and twice she stepped on loose stones that sent her skittering down the hill for a few seconds before she regained her balance.

As she reached the bottom she was torn. The body was tucked away just out of sight, hidden by the rocks and the curve of the cliffs. She didn't want to delay if someone was lying there on the sand, injured and unconscious, but equally she was aware of her own size and her strength. Petite in build, the extent of her normal physical activity was taking long, leisurely walks through the countryside or going on a brisk hill walk. If she did find some poor person lying injured at the base of the cliffs, she would not be able to do anything on her own except see to any superficial wounds. Her mind made up, Jane turned right rather than left and hurried back through the streets of the town to the set of rooms her parents had rented for the fortnight.

Slipping inside the house, she turned instinctively to the door of the room she shared with Cassandra. Her sister was her confidante, her partner in everything she did, but today she hesitated. Today she needed more help than her sister could provide.

Rapping on the door to her parents' room, she heard movement inside and eventually her father opened the door. He was still in his nightclothes, although he looked wide awake and Jane could see he had been attending to some letters by the open curtains and the scatter of papers on the small writing desk by the window.

"Jane, is something amiss?"

Before she could answer, her mother appeared, bleary-eyed. "What has happened, Jane?" There was a note of worry in her voice and Jane wished she could spare her mother the horror of what she thought she had seen.

"I need your help, Father. I am worried someone has been hurt," Jane said, trying to convey the urgency of her message without causing panic.

"Who has been hurt, Jane?"

"I do not know. I went for a walk along the cliffs this morning and I saw someone on the beach. They weren't moving. I am going to check on them, but if they are injured I will not be able to move them on my own."

Jane's clergyman father had always been good in a crisis, and he immediately went back inside his room to pull on his clothes.

"You should stay here, Jane," her mother said. Mrs Austen was protective of all her children, but especially her two daughters. Despite both Jane and Cassandra being well into adulthood, their mother still felt they needed her to shield them from the world.

"No," Jane said, shaking her head. A few years earlier she would have found it much more difficult to defy her mother's suggestion, but she had experienced much of the world these last few years and had learned that people often didn't argue if you said no with confidence. "I shall wake Cassandra."

"Do not drag your sister into this too," Mrs Austen said, this time with a note of warning in her voice.

"Hush dear," Mr Austen said as he ran a hand through his unruly hair. "There is nothing to drag Cassandra into, just the need to do our Christian duty and go to someone who may be injured or worse."

Jane mouthed a silent *Thank you* to her father and quickly went to rouse Cassandra.

She hesitated for a moment, always reluctant to wake her sister when she slept so peacefully, but the thought of whoever it was lying unmoving on the beach spurred her on and she shook her sister gently by the shoulders.

"Cassandra, get up, get dressed."

"Jane? What has happened? Your face is pale."

"I went for a walk and I think I saw someone not moving at the bottom of the cliffs. I have woken father to come and have a look with me."

"I will get dressed," Cassandra said, throwing off the bedclothes. Over the last year, since the death of her fiancé, Thomas Fowle, Cassandra had taken more of an interest in the investigations Jane undertook with the local magistrate in Hampshire, Lord Hinchbrooke. Whereas once she had cautioned Jane to avoid the potential scandal she might invite by getting mixed up in these affairs, now Cassandra was her advocate and often her companion whilst she investigated.

"Thank you, Cassandra."

Jane shifted restlessly as she waited for her father and sister to dress. Even though they only took a few minutes, when they finally emerged from their respective rooms Jane gave a sigh of relief before hurrying down the stairs and out of the door.

Moving quickly, she didn't stop to see if Cassandra and Mr Austen were keeping pace. Lyme Regis was a small town, little more than a seaside village, though it had grown in popularity in recent years as a resort for those who wanted to escape the press of the city and enjoy the restorative sea air. It would be difficult for them to get lost along the way.

There were still very few people around as they made their way to the beach. A few shopkeepers along the main street were sweeping the pavements in front of their shops, but apart from that Lyme Regis was quiet. Jane didn't hesitate to step onto the soft sand, picking up her skirts as she stepped down from the promenade but then dropping them again. Now was not the time to worry about a damp hemline.

There was no one else on the beach and as she glanced up, Jane saw the cliffs above were still empty too. As they got closer to where she thought she had seen the body, her heart rate increased and she knew it wasn't solely from the exertion. She hoped that she was wrong, that she had mistaken some debris washed up by the last tide for clothing, that her vivid imagination had filled in details that weren't there.

"Where did you see it, Jane?" Mr Austen asked, coming up to her elbow.

"A little further along," she said, as they approached the part of the beach where the cliffs jutted out a little, shielding whatever was beyond.

"You can stay here if you wish, Jane," Mr Austen said. No doubt he thought to spare her the horror of whatever she had seen lying at the base of the cliffs. These last few years he had grown to respect her as a young woman and no longer treated her like a fragile child, yet he was still her father and sought to protect her whenever he could. "You too, Cassandra."

"No," Jane said quickly. "I need to see for myself."

As they rounded the base of the cliff, Jane felt her heart skip a beat. Even from a distance it was immediately clear that what she had seen from the top of the cliff was a body.

"Lord have mercy on this poor soul," her father murmured, pausing for a second. Despite the shock, Jane moved forwards, stopping only when she was within touching distance of the corpse.

The body was that of a young woman. She lay on her front, head twisted to the side with her hair covering most of her face. Jane had been about to reach in and feel for a pulse, but it was clear this woman had been dead for some hours. Her skin had an unnatural pallor about it and her lips were blue. Hesitantly Jane brushed the hair away from the young woman's face, revealing the smooth skin and full lips. Her eyes were open, staring unseeingly into the distance, and Jane felt a deep sorrow that this young woman would never again smile or laugh or experience any of life's delights.

"Do you think she fell from the cliff?" Cassandra asked. She was standing a few feet away, holding a hand to her mouth and looking at the dead woman out of the corner of her eye. She did not shy away from difficult situations, but she was a little squeamish.

Jane did not answer, her eyes darting over the young woman's body, looking for the little clues she knew would be there.

Her clothes were well made, though not fancy. She wore a dark green, long-sleeved dress and sturdy boots. The dress was not new, but well cared for and Jane could see recent stitching along the hem. This young woman had not lived in poverty, but she could not afford to be frivolous with her clothing.

"Father, I think you should rouse the local constable," Jane said as she drew the woman's hair further back. A bloom of purple bruises had erupted on the pale skin of the young woman's neck. "I think she's been murdered."

CHAPTER TWO

There had been the predictable fierce debate about who should stay with the body and who should return to the town to alert the local constable. Mr Austen had argued that it would not be right for Jane and Cassandra to remain, but Jane had countered that it was not the first time she had seen a dead body and, besides, a constable would be more likely to listen to a man of her father's standing than a seemingly hysterical young lady. As they wanted a swift response, Mr Austen grudgingly accepted.

Jane watched him hurry off back towards the town before she crouched down again next to the body. She knew she should not disturb the young woman, even though she was keen to roll her over to look for any other injuries. A constable or magistrate would reprimand her if she disturbed the corpse too much, but she was all too aware that vital clues could be lost if they did not examine the body properly on the beach.

"Will you help me?" Jane asked, looking up at her sister.

"What do you plan to do, Jane?"

"I want to check her hands and see if we can get a better look at the bruising on her neck."

Cassandra took a step closer, crouching down next to Jane.

"See here — the bruising is in an even ring. I think these are finger marks."

"You mean she was strangled?" Cassandra said, grimacing.

"Yes." Jane nodded. "And if she was, then there will be other signs too." Lord Hinchbrooke, always eager to impart his knowledge to Jane, had recently told her how to check for signs of strangulation that might not be immediately obvious. "There can be subtle changes in the skin or eyes, petechial

12

haemorrhages," he had said. Jane leaned in closer to look at the young woman's eyes. In both there were the telltale tiny red spots that come from the bursting of the fragile small blood vessels. "When someone compresses the large vessels of the neck, they cut off the supply of blood to the brain," Jane explained, recalling what Lord Hinchbrooke had said. "But they also occlude the veins that carry the blood out of the head. The pressure in all the blood vessels increases and the small ones cannot withstand the force within them and pop, leaving these tiny red marks."

She glanced up and saw Cassandra take a couple of steps away, her face pale.

"I'm sorry," she said quickly. "That was too much detail."

Cassandra waved a hand but didn't come any closer. "I will be perfectly fine in a moment. You continue."

Jane was aware that in no time at all someone official from Lyme Regis would be hurrying along the beach and insisting she move away from the body. "Let me know if anyone starts to approach, Cassandra. I am going to have a look at her hands."

One hand was free, splayed out on the sand, but the other was tucked underneath the body, and Jane had to roll the young woman a little to release it.

Carefully she studied her hands. They were not callused, pointing to an occupation that didn't require a lot of manual labour. Most maids had rough skin on their hands from fetching and carrying and washing, and the women who worked in the fields or mending the fishing nets here in Lyme Regis would have calluses from the repetitive nature of their work.

Jane took each finger in turn, meticulously looking at the nails to see if anything was caught under them, but there was nothing she could identify.

"Poor girl," Cassandra said quietly. "Jane, people are coming."

Jane glanced over her shoulder and quickly rearranged the woman's arms as best as she could, standing up and brushing the sand off her dress before the group of people came closer.

Mr Austen was at the front, his face set in a serious expression. Three other men hurried behind. Two were past middle age and had grey hair, one with a stocky build and the other more slender. The third was young: a tall, skinny man who loped across the sand, putting Jane in mind of a goat. Even from this distance it was apparent he was nervous as he squinted ahead, trying to catch a glimpse of what lay in wait for him.

"This is Mr Margill, the local magistrate," Mr Austen said, motioning to the first of the men in the little party as they came to a stop a few feet away. "And this is Dr Woodward."

All eyes were fixed on the young woman's body, but Jane bowed her head momentarily in greeting.

"Gentlemen, these are my daughters, Miss Cassandra Austen and Miss Jane Austen. Jane spotted this unfortunate young woman's body when she was out walking on the cliffs this morning."

"Rather early to be out unaccompanied," Mr Margill murmured disapprovingly.

"I often take an early morning walk before everyone is awake."

Jane held the magistrate's eye, refusing to look away. She caught a glimpse of disdain as he regarded her.

Dr Woodward stepped forward and motioned for Jane to move aside. His expression was sombre and his demeanour frosty.

"Have you touched the body?" There was a hint of accusation in his voice and Jane wondered if the magistrate and doctor were usually this unfriendly.

"Yes, briefly," Jane said, squaring her shoulders. She refused to be intimidated. "I wanted to check if she was alive."

The doctor grunted and crouched down beside the corpse. "Quite clearly dead."

Jane felt Cassandra's warning hand on her arm and bit back the retort that was on the tip of her tongue. She glanced at the third man. Up close he was younger than she had first thought, little more than a boy, tall and gangly, but with the oversized features that hinted he hadn't quite finished growing. He had a smattering of spots across his forehead and a large Adam's apple that bobbed up and down as he swallowed.

"It is Rebecca Robertson. I recognise her," Dr Woodward said, sitting back on his haunches and shaking his head absently before he got up. "Tragic."

"Accident or suicide?" the magistrate asked.

The doctor glanced at the cliffs above and shook his head. "Difficult to say. If she was out in the dark, it would be easy for her to stumble and fall over the edge of the cliff. A fall from that height would have killed her outright."

"No," Jane said, unable to stop herself. She couldn't understand what the doctor was saying. He must have seen the bruising around her neck; he must have noticed the lack of any blood on her head or any injury that would suggest she had fallen from a great height onto the rocks below.

"Perhaps it would be best if you took your daughters back to town, Mr Austen," Mr Margill said. "It must be distressing for them to witness such a tragedy."

"She didn't fall from the cliffs," Jane said, raising her eyes to meet the magistrate's in a challenge. "And she didn't jump either."

"I hardly think you are qualified to make that assertion, Miss Austen," Mr Margill said. "Please do not concern yourself further. Dr Woodward will examine the body fully before the inquest and make his findings known."

"She has bruising around her neck and petechiae on the skin of her face. She has clearly been strangled. What is more, a fall from the cliffs, be it a deliberate jump or an accidental stumble, would result in some sort of trauma. Broken bones, or an injured skull."

Dr Woodward and Mr Margill exchanged a glance.

"You seem to know a lot about this, Miss Austen," Mr Margill said.

"Hardly," she scoffed. "Anyone with a little common sense could see that young woman was murdered."

"That is a very serious allegation to be throwing around."

Mr Austen stepped forward. "My daughter assists Lord Hinchbrooke, our local magistrate, with his duties," he said. "She has some experience in these matters."

Jane was thankful for her father's intervention, but she had dealt with enough men like Mr Margill to know he was a man of bluster.

Dr Woodward regarded her and then smiled, although it did not reach his eyes. "Miss Austen, forgive me," he said. "I was abrupt, rude even. I confess I am in shock. I have known Miss Robertson since she was a little girl. To see her lying thus on the beach, the life snuffed out of her far too prematurely, it has

16

shaken me." He took a step towards Jane and reached for her arm, as if they were the greatest of confidantes. "I do not know what happened to Miss Robertson, but you have my word that I will examine her thoroughly and report my findings to the twelve good men of the jury at the inquest."

"They will see the body too?" Jane asked. She had only been involved directly in one inquest, a case in Bath the year before where a new friend had been accused of the murder of her husband, but Jane had attended others with Lord Hinchbrooke, sitting silently and watching the proceedings. Often the body would be left where it had been found, with the magistrate taking the jurors out to view it *in situ*, undisturbed. If the death had occurred in a particularly public place, then it was up to the magistrate's discretion whether it could be moved or left where it was for everyone to gawk at.

"All correct procedures will be adhered to," Mr Margill replied stiffly. "Now, I really think it is time you returned to your lodgings. I have your address and will send someone to update you later."

"I assume you will need me as a witness at the inquest," Jane pressed. She felt uneasy about leaving this young woman here. The magistrate and doctor should be the best advocates for her now she had no voice of her own, but Jane got the distinct impression they were looking to downplay the tragedy that had happened here. Their motivations were as yet unclear. Perhaps it was to avoid panic, perhaps to prevent tarnishing the reputation of their fledgling seaside resort, or perhaps they were merely lazy and incompetent. Whatever the reason, Jane was keen to ensure everything was done correctly to give the best chance of getting justice for Miss Robertson.

"I am sure our local coroner will want you there for the inquest, Miss Austen," Mr Margill said as he ushered them away with a sweeping motion.

Jane looped her hand through Cassandra's arm and started to walk back along the beach towards Lyme Regis. For a minute all three Austens were quiet, waiting until they were out of earshot before saying anything.

"That was strange, was it not?" Jane said, looking from her father to her sister.

"Yes, that was strange," Cassandra confirmed.

"There is no rulebook in how to react when dealing with a tragedy such as this," Mr Austen said. Her father was always fair and forgiving, much like Cassandra in nature, endeavouring to give both sides of an argument equal consideration and weight.

"The doctor was trying to make out she had fallen from the cliff, when it was clear she had been strangled."

"Perhaps he did not want to offend our delicate sensibilities," said Cassandra.

Jane considered for a moment and then shook her head. "I do not think it was done to spare us."

"There will be an inquest, Jane," Mr Austen said, his voice taking on a soothing tone. "The truth will be revealed there."

Jane and Cassandra shared a look, both thinking of the last inquest they had attended in Bath where the truth had been manipulated and twisted.

"We will be there," Cassandra said, her voice firm. "We saw what had happened to that young woman, and we will not shy away from telling the truth."

"Your mother is going to be beside herself with worry," Mr Austen said as they rounded the base of the cliff and Lyme Regis came back into view.

"She will insist we return home, but I cannot do that, Father."

"I know, Jane. I will talk to your mother."

For a moment they fell silent and Jane took the opportunity to look back over her shoulder at the cliffs and the beach below.

"What are you thinking, Jane?"

"It is a remote spot, a good walk from Lyme Regis and much further from Charmouth."

"It is."

"I do not know how far the tide comes up, but I saw no evidence of anything being dragged across the sand. A body, for instance."

"You think she was killed where we found her?"

"Yes, I think it makes sense. If she was killed in the town, why not leave her body there? It isn't as though she was going to remain hidden for long. People are always walking along the cliffs above or strolling across the sands to Charmouth."

"She walked out there, in the dark?"

"I think so. Either to meet someone, or arm in arm with someone she knew and trusted."

Cassandra grimaced. "That is a horrible thought."

"She was killed by someone she knew."

"Presumably someone local."

Jane nodded and looked at her sister. "Perhaps that is why the magistrate and doctor are reluctant to admit what happened."

"It is difficult to face up to the fact someone you know is a killer."

"Jane, Cassandra," Mr Austen said, a note of admonishment in his voice. "We do not know all the facts yet. You should not speculate."

"I am sorry, Father. You are right. Gossip and supposition can be most harmful, but I would be interested to know if Miss Robertson had a young man courting her."

"Surely the guilty party would have fled by now," Cassandra said. "They must know how it would look. Especially in a small place like Lyme Regis."

"There can't be more than two hundred people living in the town, perhaps a few dozen more with the rented rooms and lodging houses now it is summer."

As they stepped up from the beach onto the short promenade, Jane paused to look at the town. She wondered if Cassandra was right and the murderer had fled, or if they were secreted in one of the houses, peering out of the window as events unfolded.

CHAPTER THREE

"Please stop pacing, Jane. My nerves cannot take it any longer." Mrs Austen stood abruptly, placing a restraining hand on her youngest daughter's arm.

"I am sorry, Mama," Jane said affectionately, but she felt on edge and couldn't sit still. It was past three in the afternoon, and all day they had waited in the rented rooms for the magistrate or coroner to come and question them. "I know there is much to do, but surely interviewing the people who found the body should be near the top of their list of priorities."

"Perhaps they work differently to Lord Hinchbrooke," Cassandra said, looking up from her needlework. Sometimes Jane envied her sister's calm demeanour and ability to sit quietly even when there was much excitement around her. She looked the perfect example of a demure young woman, dressed in a modest gown with her hair neatly pinned and her focus on gentle pursuits. "Perhaps they will hold the inquest in a few days, so they feel there is no need to rush to hear your recollection of events."

"Inquests are best held when all the facts are fresh," Jane murmured. She walked over to the window and peered out. The street outside was busy with local people hurrying to and fro, as well as those on holiday strolling at a more leisurely pace. The day was warm and sunny, perfect weather for visiting the seaside. "I am going out," Jane declared suddenly.

"Mr Margill implied he wanted us to stay in our lodgings so we would be easy to contact," Mr Austen said, looking up from the book he was reading.

"I only plan on going to look at the sea. I might even take a stroll along the Cobb. If Mr Margill comes looking for me, you can tell him that is where I will be."

"Do you think that wise, Jane?" Mrs Austen said. Over the last few years there had been a subtle shift in the relationship between Mrs Austen and her daughters. As they were unmarried, Jane and Cassandra resided at home, yet they were no longer children. Slowly they had gained more independence, travelling on occasion without their parents and making their own plans to stay with friends or family. Jane was grateful her parents were less overbearing than those of some of her acquaintances. A few years earlier her mother would have forbade her from stepping out for a walk around Lyme Regis, but now she merely hinted she thought it a bad idea.

"I do not think I can bear to stay inside any longer, Mama. I am plagued by the image of that poor young woman and I need to fill my mind with something else."

"I will accompany you, Jane," Cassandra said, setting down her needlework. "The town is tiny. If the magistrate calls then he will find us easily enough."

Before any further objections could be raised, Jane picked up her bonnet and headed for the door, only pausing outside to wait for her sister to catch up.

They walked arm in arm through the streets that led to the promenade. It was another hot day and Jane was thankful for the shade from her bonnet as they stepped out from the shade of the narrow streets toward the sea. The sun was reflected off the water, making it shimmer and sparkle, and the scene in front of them looked as if it could be from a painting. Little fishing boats bobbed in the harbour, the fishermen back from their day's work. Above their heads seagulls squawked and flapped, swooping for food, and fashionable couples walked arm in arm along the harbour wall.

Jane took a deep breath, trying to let go of some of the tension that had been building as she had paced the sitting room of their lodgings. It felt good to be out in the fresh air, to feel the gentle sea breeze on her skin. To her left the beach swept dramatically round in the direction of Charmouth, the sand golden in the afternoon light.

"I do not like it," Jane declared as they ascended the few steps onto the upper harbour wall and began to walk along it out to sea. "They should have come to question us by now."

"Perhaps, but maybe Mr Margill and the coroner have more old-fashioned views of the world. They might think they need to spare you, because you are a weak and feeble woman."

Jane snorted, a most unladylike sound that drew a shocked look from an elderly couple walking nearby. Quickly she composed herself.

"I feel pushed out."

"You cannot be involved in this, Jane. You have no connection to the deceased girl, no authority here."

Jane pondered her sister's words and knew she was correct. In Hampshire she had Lord Hinchbrooke's support, but here in Lyme Regis she was no one important. They reached the end of the Cobb and Jane leaned on the low wall, looking out to sea. It was blustery out here, the wind warm and salty. She wondered what Miss Robertson had been thinking as she hurried along the beach the night before, whether she was excited to meet a friend or lover, or scared that she was heading into a dangerous situation.

"Let us go and see the doctor," Jane said, straightening up.

"The doctor?"

"He will be easy to find, any local will be able to direct us to his house, and he will know what is happening."

"I do not think it would be appropriate, Jane."

"Nonsense. It is natural to be interested in the fate of the girl we found dead on the beach. It would be strange if we did not make enquiries."

Jane felt her resolve deepen and linked her arm through Cassandra's. They would start with Dr Woodward, and if he would not tell them anything, she was sure she would be able to track down either the magistrate or the coroner.

They walked back along the Cobb, skirts whipping around their legs in the wind. At the end of the harbour wall, Jane glanced around. Everyone was going about their business as normal and it suddenly struck her as odd. In London it was not unusual for a body to be found floating in the Thames after a drunken brawl, but here in the sleepy little seaside resort of Lyme Regis she doubted there had been another murder in living memory. People should have been aghast, stopping their neighbours on street corners to talk about it, to speculate about what had occurred. Lyme Regis was small enough that most of the residents would be known to one another; opinions on the culprit would abound.

There was none of that. No gossiping, no expressions of sadness or glances of fear.

"Does it strike you as odd, Cassandra, how people are acting?"

Cassandra's brow creased. "I do not see what you mean, Jane. Nothing is out of the ordinary."

"One of their own has been killed, yet all is continuing as usual. Think of Steventon when Miss Roscoe was murdered. No one could talk of anything else for weeks. Steventon and all the neighbouring villages stopped work on the day of her funeral. Yet here, no one is even talking about the recent tragedy."

Cassandra looked around and nodded slowly. "You are right. It is strange."

A little to their left were two middle-aged women, strolling along and enjoying the sea air. They did not appear to be in a hurry, but something about the casual way they walked and talked made Jane think they were locals rather than visitors to the seaside resort.

"Excuse me," Jane said, offering her most friendly smile. "I am sorry to trouble you, but do you know where Dr Woodward lives?"

"He has a house on Coombe Street. I am not sure of the number, but it is the largest house on the street and has steps up to the front door," one of the ladies said. "He may be out doing house calls at this time, but he has a housekeeper who will take messages for him if needed."

"Thank you," Jane said.

"If you walk for a minute in that direction, and take a right and then the next left, you will find Coombe Street," the second woman said.

Jane and Cassandra gave their thanks and then hurried away. It was easy to navigate their way through the streets and soon they were standing outside the largest house on Coombe Street, looking up at the front door.

"He might refuse to see us," Cassandra said.

"There is only one way to find out."

Jane climbed the six steps and rapped on the door, hearing movement inside after a few seconds. The door was opened by a small woman, dressed in a smart black dress with a high collar and long sleeves. It looked to be a very warm piece of clothing for such a hot day.

"Can I help you?"

"We are looking for Dr Woodward," Jane said.

"Dr Woodward isn't here. He has been called away to Exeter."

Jane recoiled in surprise. Exeter was near on thirty miles away and would take a couple of days' hard riding to reach and the same for a return journey.

"What?"

The housekeeper looked Jane up and down, disdain on her face. "Who are you?"

"Miss Jane Austen, and this is my sister, Miss Cassandra Austen."

"Are you patients of Dr Woodward?"

"We met him this morning when we found the body on the beach."

The housekeeper's eyes narrowed and Jane saw her hand twitch on the door.

"Dr Woodward isn't here," she repeated. "He will not be back for a few days. If you need a doctor, I suggest you try Dr Williams in Charmouth." She began to push the door closed, only stopping when Jane's arm shot out and held it open.

"Why has he gone to Exeter?"

"That is none of your business."

The housekeeper gave the door a final push and closed it abruptly, almost sending Jane sprawling down the stairs.

"How rude," Jane muttered, looking up at the closed door with a frown on her face. "This is strange, is it not? Dr Woodward should be examining a dead body for the coroner, and instead he is on his way to Exeter."

"It does seem strange, but perhaps there is an innocent explanation. Dr Woodward might have been called to a family emergency; his housekeeper would be under strict instructions

26

not to give out personal information to strangers," Cassandra said, ever the voice of reason.

Jane nodded. "I suppose the doctor from Charmouth might have been asked to step in to help with the inquest. Let us enquire of the magistrate."

They walked away from the doctor's house, heading back to the main street and entering a haberdashery they had spent some time in the day before.

"Miss Austen and Miss Austen, what a pleasure to see you again," Mrs Patterson said as she bustled out from the back room. She was approaching sixty, her grey hair swept back from a cheerful face with rosy cheeks that made her look as though she had been spending too much time by the fire.

"Good afternoon, Mrs Patterson. I trust you are well today?" Cassandra said.

"Yes, thank you, my dear. I was just getting ready to close up the shop. It has been dreadfully quiet today, but it is often like that with the warm weather. Everyone wishes to be out on the beach or walking along the cliffs, not looking at ribbons and bows."

"We came in to ask a favour, Mrs Patterson," Jane said.

"Oh yes, anything I can help you with would be my pleasure."

"We are looking for the local magistrate, Mr Margill. We wondered if you knew where he lived?"

"He lives at Sea View House, on the Sidmouth Road. It is a large house with wrought iron gates and a long driveway — impossible to miss."

"Is it far from Lyme Regis?"

"No, it will take about fifteen minutes to walk there. I do not mean to pry, but is something amiss?"

Jane considered for a moment and then leaned in closer. She was eager to know what Mrs Patterson had heard about the death on the beach. "We need to speak to him about the young woman who was found dead this morning."

"Ah yes, poor Miss Robertson."

"You heard about it?"

"Yes, a friend of mine came into the shop an hour ago and told me she had been found at the base of the cliffs. Poor girl, and her poor family. She must have slipped and fallen. The cliffs are beautiful, but they can be treacherous."

Jane exchanged a glance with Cassandra. "Why do you think she fell?"

"You wondered if she jumped?" Mrs Patterson shook her head firmly. "I know the Robertson family, and I don't think that likely at all. They are good people, godly people, and young Miss Robertson was a happy, bright creature, always smiling. It is a tragedy that a young life has been cut short by such an accident, but an accident it was. The coroner said as much."

Jane's head jolted up. "The coroner?"

"Sir Phillip Potter. I think he's from somewhere near Dorchester."

"They've had the inquest already?"

"Yes, this morning I believe. Such a relief for Miss Robertson's family for the matter to be resolved as soon as possible. They can arrange the funeral and focus on mourning that poor girl."

"You are sure the inquest happened this morning?" Jane asked, a sharp note in her voice that made the shopkeeper look up in surprise.

"Oh yes, but it is not unusual. I think they always try to see to these matters as soon as possible. We had a young woman drown six weeks ago; her body washed up on the beach, and it was much the same then. The inquest was held the same morning, and her family buried her the next day."

"Thank you for your help, Mrs Patterson," Cassandra said, touching Jane's arm to bring her out of her reverie. "We should return to our rooms. Our parents will be waiting for us."

They walked quickly from the shop. Jane turned to her sister, eyes ablaze.

"They've had the inquest already."

"We do not know that for sure."

"It is why no one is gossiping about this death. They have been told it was an accident and they have no reason to doubt the men in authority."

"Slow down, Jane," Cassandra said, catching hold of her sister's arm.

"We cannot return to our rooms yet." Jane felt a fire spark inside her, a sense of purpose that she knew would not easily be squashed.

"The magistrate will not like us turning up at his house unannounced."

"I'm not suggesting we go to see the magistrate. I think instead we should call on the Robertson family."

"They'll be in shock, Jane."

"If they are being lied to, they deserve to know."

"Now? Before we have all the facts to hand?"

"It is the only way, Cassandra."

CHAPTER FOUR

The Robertsons lived in a modest house on the outskirts of Lyme Regis. It was set back from the street and had a pretty front garden, filled with colourful summer plants. The house itself looked freshly painted and well kept, and Jane paused to look up at it, wondering what Mr Robertson's occupation was. Many of the dwellings in Lyme Regis were small, the abodes of fishermen and their families, people who barely scraped the rent together each month, but this was a step up in size and comfort.

Jane clasped Cassandra's hand before she approached the door. "I promise we will not overstay our welcome. Any sign that our presence is causing the family undue distress and we will leave."

Cassandra nodded and Jane turned back to the house, feeling suddenly nervous now it was time to talk to the deceased woman's family. They might refuse her entry and report to the magistrate that she was pestering them when all they wanted to do was grieve.

Summoning her courage, she pushed through the wooden gate and knocked on the front door, catching the scent of the roses that grew to one side. They were beautiful pink blooms, their fragrance sweet, and for a moment Jane was transported back to the rectory garden in Steventon. Her favourite bench was by a rose bush very much like this one, and she had spent many an hour sitting contemplating her current manuscript as the bees buzzed around the flowers.

The door opened almost immediately and Jane was surprised to be confronted by the smart red uniform of the militia. A young man of around twenty-five looked down at her with a frown.

"This is not a good time," he said, starting to close the door before Jane could utter a single word.

Jane stuck a hand out, aware she was overstepping the boundaries of propriety, but not wanting another door closed in her face.

"My name is Miss Jane Austen," she said quickly. "I was the one who found Miss Robertson this morning, on the beach."

The young man hesitated and then took a step back, motioning for her and Cassandra to step inside.

There was a small hall with a room off to either side, both doors closed. There was the faint sound of voices from the room on the left and the occasional sob. The young man led them instead to the room on the right.

It was set up as a study, with a desk under the window and a shelf of books to the left of the mantlepiece. The room was small, barely big enough for the three of them, but the young man closed the door behind them anyway.

"I am Samuel Robertson," he said quietly. "Rebecca is my sister."

"I am sorry for your loss," Jane murmured.

He looked at her with sorrowful eyes and when he spoke again, his voice was barely more than a whisper. "As you can imagine, Miss Austen, my mother is distraught. We all are. I cannot fathom how disturbing it must have been to find my sister at the base of the cliffs this morning, but I think it would be for the best if you did not burden my mother with the knowledge you have of Rebecca's death."

Jane nodded. He wanted to spare his mother any unnecessary details of her daughter's death, which was understandable.

"I will not trouble your mother, if you think that for the best," Jane said.

"Thank you, Miss Austen." He moved to open the door.

"I understand the inquest has been held already?"

"Yes, we are grateful the coroner and magistrate organised everything so quickly."

"It is good of them," Jane said, her eyes fixed on the handsome young man. He ran a hand through his hair and his shoulders sagged, as if he carried the weight of the world on them. "Did they tell you what the verdict was?"

"Accidental death," Samuel Robertson said, opening the door to show them out. "I do not like to imagine her last moment, plummeting from the clifftop, but Dr Woodward assured us her death would have been quick."

Jane glanced at Cassandra and saw her sister's worried face, realising now was her last chance to say something before they were ushered from the house.

"I do not think your sister's death was accidental," Jane said, louder than she had meant to, the words tumbling out in a rush.

At first Samuel Robertson didn't react, his expression blank, but then he shook his head and rounded on her. "I do not know who you are or what your motivations are, Miss Austen, but my family are grieving. Please leave before you add to their pain."

"It is not my intention to cause hurt, Mr Robertson, but I am worried a lie has been told here. I saw your sister's body and I know she did not fall from the cliff."

"Out!" Mr Robertson demanded, flinging open the front door. Cassandra linked her arm through Jane's and almost pulled her out of the door and into the front garden.

"What is going on? Who are these people, Sam?"

Jane turned to see the door to the left of the hall had been opened and a dishevelled woman was peering out, a girl of about thirteen or fourteen at her elbow, taking in the scene with curiosity.

"No one, Mother. They are leaving."

"Please," Jane said, desperate for them to listen to her. The last thing she wanted to do was add to the grief they were feeling, but there was something underhand going on and they deserved to know what had truly happened. "Please listen to me."

"Sam?" Mrs Robertson said, looking at her son for guidance.

"Go!" Samuel Robertson said, raising his voice to ensure they knew it brooked no argument.

Jane broke free from Cassandra's grip on her arm and stepped quickly to the young man's side, dropping her voice so the women inside the house could not hear.

"Your sister had bruising around her neck. You do not get that from a fall from a cliff. I do not know why the officials are covering this up, but they are not telling you the truth." She darted away as soon as she had finished speaking, hurrying into the street and walking briskly away with Cassandra. Her heart was pounding, and her head throbbed with every step she took.

"That did not go well," she said eventually.

"No." Cassandra looked grim. "I do not think you are going to succeed here, Jane. No one is going to believe us when we tell them what we saw. We will be dismissed as two hysterical young women."

Jane contemplated this morosely as they slowed to a more sedate pace.

They walked in silence back to their rented rooms, neither in the mood for talking. Jane thought of the despair on Mrs

Robertson's face, the horror and grief that would plague the woman for the rest of her life. Perhaps the magistrate and coroner were trying to spare the Robertsons the horror of knowing what had happened to their beloved Rebecca, but if there was a murderer at large then surely finding them and bringing them to justice had to override any desire to protect the family from the truth.

"Jane? Cassandra? Whatever is the matter?" Mrs Austen said as she ushered them in. "You look terrible."

"No one thinks there has been a murder," Cassandra said, glancing at Jane. Jane motioned for her sister to explain, suddenly exhausted by the events of the day. She wanted to crawl between the sheets of her bed and let sleep take her. "They had the inquest this morning, apparently. They have told the family it was an accidental death."

Mr Austen shook his head. "That's not right. Even I could see that was no accident."

"Perhaps it is for the best," Mrs Austen said. She must have seen Jane's expression, for she held her hands up in a placating gesture. "I do not mean an incorrect verdict is for the best, but merely that this is not our concern, Jane. This is for the local authorities to deal with, and perhaps it is best that they settle everything without involving you."

"They are ignoring a murder," Jane said bluntly. "Why, I do not know, but a woman has been killed and the truth deserves to be brought to light."

"This is not your fight, Jane. You do not know anyone here. Let the magistrate deal with things."

Jane turned, unable to summon the energy to fight her mother on this matter.

"I am tired," she said, pressing a hand to her forehead. "I think I need to rest. Perhaps we could talk about it in the morning, Mama."

"Of course, Jane. Both of you rest and tomorrow we will discuss our plans for going home."

Jane would not be going home, of that she was sure, but this evening she would not make reasoned or sensible arguments to the contrary.

Across the hall Jane and Cassandra entered their bedroom in silence, sitting down to kick off their shoes. Jane flopped back onto the bed, groaning, one hand pressed against her forehead. Never had she come across a situation like this where everyone seemed intent on denying a crime had occurred.

"Tomorrow is a new day, Jane," said Cassandra. "Try to get some rest and put this awful matter from your mind for a few hours."

"It is impossible," Jane murmured. Before she could say anything more, there was a sharp rap on the door.

Jane stood, crossing to the door and opening it, expecting to see one of her parents outside. Instead it was Mrs Riley, the woman who owned the rooms they were renting for a few days for their stay at the seaside.

"You have a visitor," she said, a frown on her face. "You may use the sitting room downstairs if you wish, as there are no visitors allowed in the rooms."

"Thank you, Mrs Riley," Jane said, casting a bemused look at Cassandra.

"I do not know what he is doing here. It isn't proper, not on such a day," Mrs Riley said as she turned to walk away.

"Who is the visitor, Mrs Riley?" Jane called after her.

The older woman turned back to answer. "The young Robertson lad. I do not know what he is thinking. He should be with his mother."

She disappeared along the hall, leaving Jane and Cassandra to quickly hurry after her.

"Leave the door open. I will have no question of impropriety in my house," Mrs Riley said as they reached the set of public rooms she allowed the guests to use.

"No doubt so she can listen in," Jane murmured, before pushing the door open.

Sam Robertson was standing in front of the mantelpiece, hands clasped together in front of him, looking uneasy. By his side was the young girl they had seen at the Robertsons' house earlier that afternoon.

"Thank you for agreeing to meet with me," Samuel Robertson said, taking a step forwards, a worried expression on his face.

Cassandra pushed the door almost to a close, leaving only the tiniest sliver of space between it and the frame.

"Mr Robertson, I must say I am surprised to see you," Jane said, remembering the rage on his face as he had ordered them from his mother's house. He was still dressed in his smart military jacket, each button shined to perfection and the fabric brushed so it looked almost new.

"I apologise for my previous behaviour. I was in shock, but it does not excuse how I spoke to you." His voice was quiet but precise and spoke of a good education.

"Please do not concern yourself," Jane said, motioning for their guests to have a seat. "We understand the strain you are under."

"This is my sister, Miss Francesca Robertson." The girl looked tired and drawn, with a pale complexion and dark rings under her eyes. Ringlets of brown hair framed her face and she still wore her hemline short, an inch or two above the ankle.

"Is there something we can help you with, Mr Robertson?"

"Captain," Francesca corrected them, flicking her eyes up at Jane before returning her gaze to her lap. "My brother is Captain Robertson."

"Of course, please excuse my mistake."

"We're very proud of him," Francesca said and then pressed her lips together.

"Is there something we can help you with, Captain Robertson?" Jane repeated.

"Earlier, when you came to the house," he began, choosing his words carefully, "you said Rebecca's death was no accident, that you had seen her body and she had bruising around her neck."

Jane nodded, her eyes fixed on the captain's face. He was finding this difficult, and she realised he must have had great affection for his sister. "That is correct."

"I couldn't believe it at the time, but when you left and we had settled our mother, Francesca asked to speak to me. She too had heard your words."

Jane considered the pair sitting in front of her. Samuel Robertson was about a decade older than his younger sister, but he had not dismissed her concerns, instead taking the time to find out where Jane and Cassandra were staying so he could come and ask them himself.

"You believe us?"

"I do not know, it seems hard to fathom. Mr Margill, our local magistrate, came to the house personally to tell us of Rebecca's death this morning. He said she had been found on the beach and it looked as though she had fallen from the cliff. Later he returned and told us they had just held the inquest…"

"They did not invite you to attend?" Jane interrupted.

"No, there was never any suggestion of that."

Normally, the family of the deceased were expected to attend an inquest, or at the very least send a representative, for often their evidence would be needed to help the jurors decide what verdict to deliver.

"What did he tell you about the inquest?"

"Just that there was a verdict of accidental death, that they thought my sister had slipped and fallen from the cliff, and that they had arranged for her body to be taken to the undertaker who would prepare her for burial. He said he wanted to make things as easy for us possible as us."

"What makes you question the truth in what Mr Margill told you?"

Sam Robertson looked at his sister, who hesitated for a moment before replying.

"Rebecca wouldn't tell me who she was going to meet last night, but she did tell me where she was going. The last few weeks she has been sneaking out to meet someone after Mother has retired to bed. They always meet on the beach, far away from prying eyes in the town. We've lived here for all our lives, and Rebecca knew not to go up on the cliffs at night. They're treacherous and she wasn't a fool."

"Last night, when she sneaked out, she told you she was going to the beach?" Jane asked.

"Yes. She was going to meet her man on the beach at midnight. The tide was on the turn about ten, and she said it would be perfect for a romantic stroll in the moonlight."

Jane sat back in her chair and took a moment to let Francesca's words sink in.

"Francesca is right; my sister knew not to go on the cliffs after dark. The path goes close to the edge in places, and it would be all too easy to lose your footing," Samuel said. "What do you think happened to my sister, Miss Austen?"

"I think she went to meet her gentleman friend on the beach and then he strangled her and left her by the base of the cliffs." The words were blunt, but Jane didn't want any ambiguity.

"Why would Mr Margill and the coroner cover this up?"

"That is a very good question," Jane murmured.

"And Dr Woodward," Cassandra said from her position by the window. "He saw those marks on Miss Robertson's neck, he knew what had happened, yet he has allowed a verdict of accidental death to go through. Now he is in Exeter and can't be asked any awkward questions."

Sam Robertson looked defeated. He had collapsed back into the cushions and his pristine uniform was looking a little rumpled. "What do we do, Miss Austen?" he said, turning bewildered eyes onto Jane.

"Exactly what they do not wish us to do. We make a fuss until they cannot deny what has happened. Only then will they be forced to admit the truth."

Cassandra leaned forwards and held out a hand of caution. "We must remember the Robertsons have to continue to live here, Jane," she said softly. "It is all very well for us to make an enemy of the local magistrate, but that may not be a wise course of action for Captain Robertson."

"No," Samuel Robertson said quickly, "I want justice for Rebecca. She was an innocent, and my mother deserves to know the truth." He looked expectantly at Jane. "We're in your hands, Miss Austen. What do we do?"

CHAPTER FIVE

It was barely past nine o'clock, yet Jane had already been up for four hours. She had spent a restless night tossing and turning, and she had been glad when it was time to get up and start the day.

She had slipped from their rented rooms early to avoid the discussion of whether they should leave Lyme Regis with her mother, and taken a walk along the Cobb to clear her head before proceeding to the meeting point she had agreed with Captain Robertson the day before. Instead of the bright red jacket that marked him out as a soldier, he was wearing a white shirt and brown jacket, still impeccably smart but less noticeable amongst all the other people in the streets of Lyme Regis.

"Good morning, Miss Austen," he said, his voice low and serious.

"Good morning, Captain Robertson."

"Are you ready to leave?"

"I am."

"The walk will take a little less than an hour."

He led the way to the path that led to the cliffs, worn deep by the footfalls of thousands of people over the years walking from Lyme Regis to Charmouth. There was no undertaker in Lyme Regis, and after the inquest the magistrate had informed Captain Robertson that his sister's body had been transported to Charmouth to be prepared for burial. Samuel and Jane had agreed the evening before to take a walk over to Charmouth and drop in on the undertaker unannounced, so that the captain could see his sister's body for himself before they spoke to the magistrate and coroner.

"Have you been in the army long?"

"Five years," Captain Robertson said, smiling at her surprised expression. "My mother always tells me I have a youthful face," he added with a wry smile. "I was very fortunate that Lord Willingham, our local landowner, offered to buy me a commission. Men of my social status do not often become officers. I am thankful every day for the opportunity."

"That is very generous."

"My father worked for many years for Lord Willingham on his estate. I grew up around Lord Willingham's sons; we would play together in the summer when they were back from school. We grew apart, of course; their lives are a world apart from my own. My father died when I was eighteen and Lord Willingham offered then to pay for my commission."

"He must have valued your father very much."

"He did. It was a kindness that has changed the course of my life and helped to keep my mother and sisters housed in relative comfort."

It was quite a responsibility for a man so young to become the head of the family, although Jane knew of many similar stories. It was fortunate that Samuel Robertson had been old enough to seek employment when his father had died, meaning his family were provided for. Not all families were as lucky.

"You are on leave at the moment?"

"Yes, three weeks. I only returned home a few days ago." He fell silent as they climbed the path, following the same route Jane had taken the morning before.

"Do you get much opportunity to return home?"

"Less than I would like. I have only seen my mother and sisters a handful of times these last few years." He shook his head sadly. "I knew nothing about this gentleman Rebecca was sneaking out of the house to meet. Perhaps if I had been here…"

"Please do not berate yourself, Captain. It only serves to torture your soul."

"You are right of course, Miss Austen," he said, a tight smile on his face. "I feel guilty that I was not home more, but it was not my choice. A life in the army is not your own. You are confined to the whims and the will of the officers above you in rank."

"Do you enjoy your career?"

"Very much so. I love the routine and the discipline, and the camaraderie with the men. Army life is not for everyone, but I have found it suits me very well."

"I am glad to hear it. Two of my brothers are in the navy and they speak of it with much the same fondness as you. They talk of the monotony of their days at sea, but for them it is worth it for the excitement that will often follow in skirmishes. I do not think any grand sum of money would make them give up their careers in the navy and return to shore for good."

"It is a peculiar life, but one I would not change."

"You are not married, Captain Robertson?"

"No, there has never been the right circumstance, and besides, I do not know if my modest salary could support my mother and sisters — sister, I should say now — as well as a wife and family of my own."

Jane nodded, realising how much responsibility this young man carried.

They were strolling along the cliff now and approaching the spot where Jane had first spied Rebecca Robertson's body. The beach looked a long way below them, and she felt her legs tremble a little as she peered over the cliff, despite normally having a good head for heights.

"Would you tell me about your sisters, Captain Robertson?"

"Of course, although you must remember I have not spent much time at home during the last few years."

"I would still like to hear of them."

"Rebecca was always strong-willed, but quietly so. She was the sort of person who, if told that something was impossible, would focus all of her attention on achieving it. She loved books, and had a way with words that meant her letters were a joy to read. But often she was far too trusting. She was just seventeen, and saw the best in everyone." He broke off and shook his head. "I suppose that is what got her killed. Trusting the wrong person."

"Perhaps," Jane said, seeing the pain in his eyes. " Did she step out with anyone you knew, or mix much with local society?"

"To be truthful I do not know, Miss Austen. When I was home on leave she was quite content to stay in and talk in the evenings by the fire, but I do not know much about how her life was when I was away."

"Of course not." Jane suspected Francesca, the younger sister, might be a better source of information when it came to Rebecca's friendships and social life.

They walked in silence for a few minutes. The views over to Charmouth were spectacular, with the sea shimmering in the sunshine and the dark cliffs contrasting against the lush green grass above. The little town of Charmouth was set in a natural dip between two sets of cliffs, where the beach was wide and the land beyond gently sloping.

"Do your sisters attend a school?"

"Yes, at least Francesca does, and up until a year ago Rebecca did as well. Miss Warkworth's School for Young Ladies. It is a small establishment in Charmouth; they would walk over every morning and back after lessons."

"They did not board there?"

"No. They were there on the generosity of the Willingham family. As well as buying my commission, Lord Willingham put aside some money for my sisters' education. Rebecca spent three years at the school and Francesca will do the same. The money would have stretched to boarding, but my mother wanted my sisters to come home each evening. I think there are twelve pupils in total, half of whom board."

Jane nodded, thinking back to her time at school. She had gone with Cassandra after months of begging her parents to send her a year early. The idea of Cassandra going away to study without her had nearly broken her heart, and she had been determined to attend alongside her older sister. It had been a strange time, with newfound freedom for the two young Austen sisters, and she had been sad when that period of her life had come to an end.

"Since leaving school, had Rebecca mentioned any particular young man she was interested in marrying?"

"No. She spent her time with my mother, learning how to run a household and doing chores." He shrugged. "I thought it would not be long before she married, but in truth I had not given the matter much thought."

"Tell me about Francesca."

Captain Robertson smiled indulgently and Jane could see the affection he had for his youngest sibling.

"Francesca is thirteen years old and a force of nature. She is interested in everything. Rebecca enjoyed her time at school because it got her out of Lyme Regis, but Francesca really appreciates the education she receives."

"She is academic?"

"Very much so. Both of my sisters are clever." He paused and pressed his lips together before correcting himself. "*Were* clever."

Jane fell silent for a moment, allowing him time to master his grief.

"Francesca has lofty aspirations." Captain Robertson paused and then pointed to the town of Charmouth that was coming into view. "Pretty, is it not? There is quite a rivalry between Lyme Regis and Charmouth. I've never quite understood why, but there is fierce competition between our fishermen and theirs, and during the midsummer celebrations the tug of war and other games can become quite heated."

"It is beautiful. You live in a picturesque part of England." Jane paused and then pushed on with her questioning. Captain Roberts seemed willing to talk about Rebecca, and she knew there might not be another opportunity to discuss her with him. "So, there were no plans for Rebecca to marry?"

"No, though she had a small dowry. Francesca too."

"A dowry?"

"Yes, courtesy of Lord Willingham. He has been most generous. We hoped it might allow Rebecca to marry someone who could give her a comfortable life."

Jane raised her eyebrows in surprise. The Robertsons were not poor, they lived in a modest but comfortable house and it did not sound as though they struggled for the day to day necessities, but much of their good fortune had come from the generosity of Lord Willingham, for whom the late Mr Robertson had worked.

"Lord Willingham seems to be very invested in the happiness of your family."

"Yes, we would have been in quite different circumstances without him."

They started the descent down to Charmouth, the path winding away from the cliff and down the hill into the town. It was much like Lyme Regis with its narrow streets and quaint little cottages. There had been some building in the last few years, expanding the size of the town from a small settlement to something a little larger, no doubt to cater for the surge in visitors, as had become the fashion in recent times.

The undertaker's shop was tucked out of the way, the entrance located in an alley between two rows of shopfronts. Captain Robertson knocked on the door and they heard a shuffling sound from inside.

A small boy with a thin face opened the door. He regarded them warily.

"I am Captain Robertson. You have my sister here, Miss Rebecca Robertson. Is your master in?"

"Master is abed," the boy said.

"Rouse him. I wish to speak to him and view my sister's body."

The boy hesitated, a look of fear in his eyes. Jane caught sight of bruises on his wrist and wondered if he was poorly treated by the undertaker. Children who worked as shop boys or in the stables or kitchens of some great house were often orphans and had no one to protect them from the cruelties of their masters.

After a moment he disappeared into the darkness of the shop, closing the door behind him. Jane had begun to wonder if he was going to come back, when the door opened again to reveal a large man with tousled hair who looked as if he had just risen from his bed.

"Captain Robertson, please excuse the delay. My name is Mr Winters; how may I be of service?" The undertaker's jowls wobbled as he spoke, and he squinted at them as if he needed spectacles to see properly.

"Good morning, Mr Winters. I would like to see my sister," Captain Robertson said.

"Ah yes, of course. Please come inside."

He led them through a dark passageway to a dimly lit room beyond. The only natural light came from a small window high up in the wall, and as Jane's eyes adjusted to the gloom, she saw a coffin laid out on a workbench.

"Please accept my condolences for your loss," Mr Winters said, his head bobbing up and down nervously.

"Thank you. Is she here?"

Mr Winters cleared his throat, started to speak and then paused to clear his throat again. "Mr Margill, the magistrate, arranged for your sister's body to be brought here," he said, his eyes flicking between Captain Robertson and Jane. "He suggested I should get on with my work quickly, and I nailed down the lid of the coffin last night."

"That is unusual, is it not, Mr Winters?" Jane said quickly. "Normally the coffin is left open so the family can view the deceased's body, should they wish."

Mr Winters spread his hands and puffed out his chest. "I was only following orders."

"Orders?"

"Mr Margill suggested I should nail down the coffin as soon as I was done preparing the body." He glanced at Captain Robertson. "I took good care of her, Captain, made sure everything was done right."

"Why did Mr Margill want you to nail down the coffin?" Captain Robertson asked.

Mr Winters cleared his throat again. "He didn't say."

"He must have given you a reason," Jane pushed.

"No, but…" The undertaker trailed off.

The silence in the room grew until Mr Winters could take it no longer.

"I think it was because of the bruising," Mr Winters said quickly, the words tumbling out. "There is bruising around Miss Robertson's neck, not something I could easily cover. Even a high neck would not cover it. I assumed Mr Margill wanted to spare the family the pain of having to see that."

"Bruising?" Captain Robertson said. The colour had drained from his face.

"I think you had better show us, Mr Winters," Jane said.

"No, I can't do that, Miss. Mr Margill will be furious."

Captain Robertson let out a low, guttural sound halfway between a groan and a growl and pushed past the undertaker. He cast about the room until he found what he was looking for, picking up a small hammer with a curved end and using this to start prying open the coffin.

"Please, Captain, you'll damage the wood."

"To hell with the wood!"

Jane stood watching, unable to take her eyes off the terrible scene for a moment before springing forward. "Captain," she said, gently, laying a hand on his arm. She gave a meaningful look to Mr Winters. "Finish it," she instructed, her voice quiet but firm.

After a moment's hesitation, Mr Winters took the hammer from Captain Robertson and removed the last of the nails. He placed the hammer on the side then gripped the edge of the heavy wooden lid, staggering under the weight as he lifted it.

At first Jane could not bring herself to step forwards and look into the darkness of the coffin. Only when Captain Robertson shifted was Jane able to summon up the courage to look inside.

There had been no time for niceties for Miss Robertson. She had been placed into the coffin in the same rumpled green dress she had been wearing when Jane had found her on the beach, her hair a mess of tangles about her shoulders. No one had been allowed to lovingly comb out her tresses or dress her in her best Sunday dress.

"The magistrate…" Mr Winters began as Captain Robertson let out a sharp exhalation.

"Do not speak," the captain ordered. He reached into the coffin and gently moved the hair from around his sister's neck. The bruises were obvious, a horrible ring of purple around her pale neck that made it quite clear Miss Robertson had died by strangulation.

For a moment no one in the room moved, and then Captain Robertson looked up, anger burning bright in his eyes.

"You will return my sister to her home."

The undertaker nodded, not even attempting to argue.

Without another word, Captain Robertson spun and strode out of the room, heading down the dark passageway and back out through the door into the alley. Jane took one last look at Miss Robertson and then quickly followed.

CHAPTER SIX

By the time Jane caught up with Captain Robertson, he was already halfway back to Lyme Regis. She was out of breath, having hitched up her skirts to run after him.

"Captain Robertson," she gasped, clutching her bonnet to her head as she drew level with him. At first she did not think he was going to stop. He was frowning, his eyes fixed on the ground in front of him. It took him a moment to register she was beside him and he immediately slowed a little.

"Miss Austen, forgive me."

"There is nothing to forgive."

"They had nailed the coffin down to hide what had been done to her," he said, shaking his head.

"You saw the marks on her neck?"

"As clear as the morning sun on the horizon." He looked at her, his expression still grim. "Why would they hide this?"

It was the same question Jane had been asking herself.

"I do not know, but I think it is one of many questions we need to ask Mr Margill."

"And the coroner."

"Yes, I was thinking about the coroner," Jane said, slowly getting her breath back now she had caught up with the captain. "I was informed he lives somewhere near Dorchester."

"That is correct. Sir Phillip Potter. I've never met the man, but I know him by reputation."

"Dorchester is quite a distance away, I believe."

"Yes, some twenty-five miles. At least a good day's ride."

"Yet he was available for the inquest mere hours after I found your sister's body on the beach."

Captain Robertson slowed for a moment, nodding. "That is odd. Even with the fastest of messengers dispatched, the coroner should not have arrived here until this evening at the earliest."

"I wonder if he is still here in Lyme Regis, or if he has returned home now his work is done," Jane mused. Captain Robertson had increased his pace again and was now striding along the cliffs. She quietly gave thanks for the long walks she enjoyed back home in Hampshire, which now allowed her to keep up.

Twenty minutes later they picked their way down the path that led back to Lyme Regis. Jane felt eyes on them as they hurried through the streets and knew there would be gossip abounding once they were out of earshot.

As they neared the neat little cottage where the Robertsons lived, Captain Robertson slowed.

"I need to tell my mother, Miss Austen. I need to warn her that Rebecca is coming home and what to expect."

"I understand."

"It may be better if I go in alone, but once I have broken the news to my mother I plan on going to confront Mr Margill. I will get an answer from him."

"I will accompany you," Jane said quickly. She could not leave the matter now; she was far too invested, and hoped Captain Robertson wouldn't suggest she stay behind.

"Thank you. I will not be long. You might like to wait in the garden; there is a bench under the apple tree at the far end."

He showed her to the garden, making sure she was settled before disappearing into the house. The bench was positioned too far away for Jane to hear the conversation inside the cottage, but it was impossible to miss the sobs that followed.

After a few minutes, Francesca Robertson slipped from the house and made her way to the bench. "Sam said he saw Rebecca," the young girl said as she took a seat beside Jane. "She had been strangled, like you said."

"Yes, I'm so sorry."

"My mother is distraught."

"It is a distressing notion. To lose a child is horrific, but to know someone else has taken them away from you must be unbearable."

Francesca sat silently for a minute then turned to Jane. "You will find out what happened to my sister, won't you, Miss Austen?"

Jane was wary of promising something she might not be able to deliver, but there was such desperation in the young girl's eyes that she found herself nodding. "Yes."

"Good. I want the person who did this to her to hang."

Jane thought of the other cases she had been caught up in over the last few years. She knew justice was never straightforward, even once you had identified the culprit, but she did not share this thought with Francesca. For now, the grieving child simply needed to know that whoever had killed her sister would pay for their crime.

"I must go to my mother, but if you need anything from me please do not hesitate to ask."

Francesca was only thirteen, but already she had a maturity that Jane did not doubt would get her through this terrible time. Tragedy affected all families differently, but children were never spared and often forced to grow up fast in its wake.

Captain Robertson was inside the house for another few minutes before emerging, his face pale and drawn. Jane gave him a moment to compose himself before she rose from the bench to join him.

"You informed your mother of what we saw at the undertaker's?"

"Yes. She didn't want to believe it."

"That is understandable."

"She cannot fathom why the official men would lie to us."

Jane glanced at him. "Shall we go and find out?"

Sea View House was situated on the Sidmouth Road, a mile outside of Charmouth. The walk was pretty and in other circumstances Jane would have enjoyed spending a morning exploring the surrounding countryside. Captain Robertson's pace was unforgiving, and Jane felt a moment of sympathy for his troops if he marched them at such a relentless speed. They spoke little on the way to Mr Margill's house and Jane was glad when the wrought iron gates came into view.

There was a sweeping drive that cut through a well-tended lawn with plenty of oak and beech trees dotted throughout the front garden. A squat, colourless house was at the end of the drive, built at some point in the last decade or so with a grey stone façade and large windows.

As they approached the front door, Jane was surprised to see it open and a footman emerge.

"My master is not accepting guests," the footman said without any pretence at pleasantries.

"I am not leaving until I see Mr Margill," Captain Robertson said, his voice low and firm.

The footman was young and well built, but no physical match for Captain Robertson, and he flicked an uncertain look back at the house.

"I will find your master and drag him outside myself if you do not go and fetch him."

The footman hesitated then hurried back inside.

"Do you think they were expecting us?" Captain Robertson asked as they waited.

"I think they were expecting me, but not you. You are much harder to ignore," Jane said.

A minute passed and then another before the front door opened and Mr Margill appeared.

"Captain Robertson, my condolences once again," he said, spreading his hands and giving a disingenuous smile. "Is there something I can help you with?"

"I think you know Miss Austen."

"Of course." The magistrate inclined his head in Jane's direction but did not meet her eye.

"We have just arrived back from Charmouth," Captain Robertson said, his voice surprisingly calm now he had the magistrate standing in front of him. "We went to view my sister's body."

"Why did you ask Mr Winters to nail down the lid to Miss Robertson's coffin?" Jane asked, stepping forwards so the magistrate could ignore her no longer.

"It is not uncommon practice when there has been an accident such as the one Miss Robertson was a victim of."

"You instructed the undertaker to nail down the lid, but nails are not so hard to remove," Jane said. "We opened the coffin." She watched the magistrate's face carefully. His eyes widened a fraction.

"I saw the bruising around my sister's neck," Captain Robertson said. "I have no medical training and yet it is clear to me that she has been strangled. Her body is on its way back to my mother's house even as we speak."

"I can assure you…"

"No more lies," Captain Robertson interrupted, his voice rising. "I want the truth, or I will shout from the rooftops what you have tried to conceal."

"Captain Robertson, I will make allowances because you are so recently bereaved, but I ask you to remember to whom you speak."

"I would not care if you were the king himself. I will have answers."

Mr Margill considered for a moment. "Very well. Step inside."

The hall was a grand room with dark panelling that would have looked at home in a much older house. On the walls were a series of portraits, serious men dressed in their finest clothing, with a large painting of Mr Margill at the bottom of the staircase.

They were directed to a door that led from the hallway, and as they entered a bright and airy room Jane was surprised to see there were other people inside.

Sitting in an upright armchair was a wiry man of about sixty. He had a sharp gaze and piercing blue eyes and looked Jane over unashamedly as she walked into the room. Pacing backwards and forwards by the window was Dr Woodward, his manner agitated.

"What do we have here, Margill?" the man in the chair asked as Mr Margill followed Jane and Captain Robertson into the room.

"This is Captain Robertson, the brother of the young woman found on the beach. Captain, this is Sir Phillip Potter, coroner for Dorset."

"I am sorry for your loss, young man. A life snuffed out in its prime is a tragic event."

"Thank you, sir," Captain Robertson said stiffly.

The older man's eyes turned to Jane and she sensed his curiosity as well as an air of authority. There was no doubt who was in charge in this room.

"And this young lady?"

"Miss Austen," Jane spoke for herself, holding the older man's eye.

"How do you do, Miss Austen? You know Mr Margill, of course, and I assume you are acquainted with Dr Woodward?" He asked the question but didn't wait for an answer. "You found Miss Robertson's body, Miss Austen?"

"I did."

"Tragic," Sir Phillip said. "A terrible waste of a young life."

They had not been invited to sit and Sir Phillip had not risen, perched in his armchair as if he were a monarch holding court, spending a little time with his subjects before moving on to more pressing matters.

"I understand you have already held the inquest, Sir Phillip," Jane said. A few years ago men like Sir Phillip would have intimidated her, but she had learned much since her partnership with Lord Hinchbrooke had begun.

"Yes. It is always best to sort these matters as quickly as possible. Miss Robertson's body has been released to the undertaker, Captain Robertson, so you can arrange your sister's funeral."

Captain Robertson was about to speak when Jane rested a hand on his arm.

"It was fortuitous that you were on hand for the inquest," Jane said mildly, holding Sir Phillip's eye. She thought he suppressed a smile at her challenge and realised that he viewed their exchange as a game, something to be won or lost.

"Fortuitous indeed."

"I understand you live near Dorchester, some twenty-five miles away."

"You are well informed, Miss Austen. Remind me what your interest in this tragic matter is?"

Jane ignored the question and instead pressed on with her gentle enquiries. "Were you visiting friends? Here on business?"

"You become impertinent, Miss Austen," Mr Margill intervened, stepping forward.

Jane looked around the room. She was surrounded by powerful men. "I apologise for any perceived impertinence," she said sweetly, looking from man to man. "I suppose I am confused as to what has happened here. I beg for an uninterrupted minute to lay out what I know, and then I will listen to your explanations."

"You have no right to ask anything," Mr Margill said hotly.

"Let Miss Austen speak, Margill," Sir Phillip said, his words cutting through the room with authority.

"When I found Miss Robertson's body on the beach yesterday morning, it was immediately apparent that she had been strangled," Jane said. She held up a hand to silence Mr Margill's protestations. "She had bruising around her neck. I have some knowledge of how such bruising develops and what other signs to look out for, such as the petechiae on the skin of the face and neck.

"In addition, she showed no signs of trauma that would have been consistent with a fall from a great height." Jane glanced over at Dr Woodward. "I mentioned my concerns at the time, and despite Dr Woodward giving me his word that he would examine Miss Robertson's body thoroughly, he clearly did not do so."

The doctor could not meet her gaze.

"Miss Robertson was strangled and then, for some reason, you hurried through the inquest without calling the witnesses you should have, without even letting the family attend. Then you came to the frankly ludicrous conclusion of accidental death by way of a fall from the cliffs."

"You have thought all this through, Miss Austen," Sir Phillip said. She could sense tension in the room, but Sir Phillip was oddly calm, as if this matter did not really concern him. "What do you conclude from it all?"

Jane hesitated and then was suddenly struck by the truth of the matter. "You are covering up a murder," she said.

"You accuse a coroner, a magistrate and a respected doctor of covering up a murder? Why would we do that?"

"This is ridiculous," Mr Margill blurted. "I refuse to listen to any more of this nonsense."

Jane ignored the magistrate, her eyes fixed on Sir Phillip. "I can only assume that you are protecting the murderer."

The room fell silent and Jane realised she was holding her breath.

"You had better sit down, Miss Austen, Captain Robertson," Sir Phillip said eventually.

Captain Robertson took a seat beside Jane on one of the sofas. He was ill at ease and Jane sensed he would rather stand to attention than sit and relax.

"You cannot mean to tell them," Mr Margill said, staring at the coroner.

"I do not think we have any other choice. I do not know Miss Austen, but she strikes me as tenacious. I suspect that if you order her out of here, the whole town will be awash with gossip by mid-afternoon."

Sir Phillip turned to face Jane and Captain Robertson.

"What I am about to tell you is known only to the people you see in this room." His voice had dropped low so no inquisitive servants could hope to hear what he was saying. "Five months ago, the body of a young woman was found on the shoreline. She was the daughter of a fisherman in Charmouth. Her body had been in the water for days and she was not in the best condition. When Dr Woodward examined her corpse there was some bruising around her neck, but as she was found with fishing nets wrapped around her, it was presumed they had caused the marks. We held an inquest and a verdict of accidental death was decided upon."

Jane glanced around the room. Mr Margill had lost some of his bravado and now sat quietly. Dr Woodward was still at the window and stared off into the distance.

"Then six weeks ago I received an urgent message from Mr Margill. Another body had been found on the beach, this time a young woman from Lyme Regis. She had only been missing for a few hours, her body was fresh and it was clear she had been strangled. Mr Margill noted the similarities between her and the young woman who was found a few months earlier and he sent an urgent messenger."

Jane nodded, a picture forming. "You realised there was a killer, preying on young women in Lyme Regis and Charmouth."

"We thought it best to make discreet enquiries, to avoid causing any unnecessary panic. At the time we thought we would have our culprit within a few days, but it was not quite as straightforward as first hoped."

"Then Miss Robertson died."

"It was undeniably similar to the first two deaths."

"That is why you were here, Sir Phillip, in Lyme Regis."

"I have been overseeing the enquiries, travelling back and forth from my home near Dorchester. I was on my way to Lyme Regis when Mr Margill rode out to inform me of Miss Robertson's death."

"You decided to keep her murder a secret as well," Jane said. She could understand the decision, but she didn't agree with it. Young women were at risk in Lyme Regis and Charmouth and they deserved to know.

As if reading her thoughts, Captain Robertson said, "You knew there was a murderer out there, but thought you would keep that information to yourselves. Instead of warning people, instead of telling them to be careful ... not to go out alone at night."

"We did not think the killer would strike again before we could apprehend them," Mr Margill said, a note of defensiveness in his voice.

"But they did, and my sister paid the price for your hubris."

Everyone was silent for a moment and Jane closed her eyes, letting the information she had just been told sink in. It was a lot to think about. Three deaths instead of one. Three murders. Three young women strangled on the beach.

"So you see, Miss Austen, Captain Robertson, there was a good reason behind our rushing through of the inquest." Sir Phillip sat back in his chair, folded his hands together neatly and rested them against his body.

Jane raised an eyebrow. They were all aware it was more than just the rushing through of the inquest. They had presented the facts to the jury in such a way as to ensure they returned a verdict of accidental death. It was a blatant misuse of the powers they had been given, and would not be looked well upon if there was a review of the judicial process. However, the coroner was a powerful man and Sir Phillip did not look particularly worried.

Sir Phillip stood up. "We have the same aim, do we not? We all wish for the killer of Miss Robertson and the two other young women to be brought to justice?"

Jane inclined her head. Beside her, Captain Robertson didn't move.

"Then I ask you to trust our judgement. Mr Margill and I will not rest until this matter is resolved and the killer brought to justice."

"You surely do not mean to keep the facts hidden?" Jane said, aware that Sir Phillip was hoping to usher her and Captain Robertson from the room with the promise they would remain silent.

"There is no sense in panicking the local community," Mr Margill said quickly. "It will muddy the waters and make the investigation harder."

"It has been six weeks since the last death, yet instead of you placing the culprit in custody Miss Robertson lost her life."

"That is regrettable," Sir Phillip murmured.

"Regrettable? It is a travesty!" Jane felt a surge of anger. As usual, a group of men were deciding what was best in a matter that predominantly affected women. "If Miss Robertson knew of this killer, then her death may have been entirely preventable."

"We cannot know that," Sir Phillip said sharply, some of his control slipping for an instant.

"My sister is dead," Captain Robertson said, cutting through the argument. "My sister is dead and you could have warned her against the danger she faced." He stood and walked over to the door, turning back to face the room. "I refuse to stay quiet and let another woman die."

He flung open the door and left the room, striding from the house before anyone could stop him.

Jane rose to follow him, getting as far as the door before Sir Phillip's voice called to detain her.

"A moment, Miss Austen. I have a proposition for you, if you would grant me the favour of listening."

CHAPTER SEVEN

Jane took her seat on the sofa again, feeling vulnerable without Captain Robertson by her side.

"Mr Margill tells me you have assisted the magistrate in Hampshire on a number of investigations," Sir Phillip said.

"That is correct. Lord Hinchbrooke has been a generous mentor."

"I know Lord Hinchbrooke a little. He is a shrewd man. You have helped him in cases such as this before?"

"Nothing quite the same, but I have been involved in a number of murder investigations."

Sir Phillip studied her for a moment. "I think your help will be invaluable here," he said.

Jane waited to hear what the coroner proposed. It was a sudden change in attitude. One moment he had been intent on keeping her in the dark, the next he seemed to be suggesting a partnership.

"Captain Robertson is understandably upset. He mourns the loss of his sister and perhaps is not able to see the intricacies of a case like this through his grief. I fear, after our exchange today, that neither Captain Robertson nor his mother are going to be pleased to have one of our agents question them about Miss Robertson."

Jane inclined her head. He was not wrong there; the coroner and magistrate were hardly going to be welcome in the Robertson household.

"You have been able to get close to the family. They trust you. I propose you support the family, ask the questions we cannot, and report our progress back to them."

Jane shifted uncomfortably. "You wish for me to betray their confidence?"

"Not at all. It need not be a secret that you are cooperating with the magistrate and myself. It may just make things more palatable for the family."

"In return you will share information with me?"

"Where we can, of course," Sir Phillip said, attempting a smile. "As part of this agreement we would ask you to persuade Captain Robertson to keep the matter quiet, of course. I am sure you can see the merits of investigating without causing any hysteria in the town."

Jane stood and smoothed down her dress. "Thank you for the offer," she said, drawing herself up to her full height. "I will of course support the Robertson family, but I will not have a part in covering up these murders. I will not put anyone else at risk."

She bobbed a quick curtsey and darted out the door, hurrying down the drive after Captain Robertson.

Jane caught him up a few minutes later. He had stopped at the side of the road and was leaning against a fence. He was breathing heavily and Jane could see tears on his cheeks. As she approached, he straightened up and quickly wiped the tears away.

"Miss Austen, I apologise for leaving you there with those scoundrels. It was unforgiveable."

"There is no need to apologise, Captain. I can see why you could not bear to spend another minute in the room with them."

"Three women," Captain Robertson said, shaking his head. "They knew there was a murderer prowling the streets and yet they told no one."

"We know the truth now," Jane said, deciding not to mention the proposal Sir Phillip had offered her. "We can spread the word and try to minimise the danger to other young women."

"It is too late for Rebecca, though."

They fell silent, and after a moment Captain Robertson offered Jane his arm and slowly they began the walk back to Lyme Regis.

"Do you think they will try to silence us? If we tell people?"

Jane considered for a moment. "No. Now we know the truth, I do not think they will deny it."

"How do I tell my mother?" Captain Robertson said, a fresh wave of despair in his voice. "How do I tell her that Rebecca's death might have been prevented?"

Jane had no answer to the question and instead squeezed his arm in solidarity.

Back in Lyme Regis, Jane was invited into the Robertson house for the second time, but on this occasion was shown into the kitchen at the back of the house. It was clear this was where the family spent most of their time. A large table was at one end of the room, with four chairs around it and a space at the other end for chopping and preparing food. Jane began to pull out a chair, but Francesca gave a little shake of the head and gestured for her to take the one next to it. The seat must have been Rebecca's. Mrs Robertson sat at the head of the table, Captain Robertson to her left and the empty chair on her right. Francesca perched on a stool at the end of the table.

For a moment Jane felt a pang of sorrow that this family would never be complete again. She couldn't remember the last time her own family had all sat around one table; with two brothers in the navy and her other brothers occupied with their own professions and families, it wasn't often that they visited Steventon at the same time. Yet her siblings were all successful and healthy, and neither of her parents showed signs of illness. They had not known the tragedy of loss like the Robertsons. First Mr Robertson had passed away, and now Rebecca. This family was forever changed, forever depleted.

"My deepest condolences," Jane said gently.

Mrs Robertson was a slender woman in her forties who was blessed with a handsome face and thick, chestnut hair. Today her eyes were red-rimmed and puffy and her cheeks drained of colour, but she still was an attractive woman and Jane wondered that she had not remarried in the years since her husband's death. It would have meant the family would not be reliant on Captain Robertson's pay as their only income.

Captain Robertson had spoken to his mother in private and told her of the other two deaths that had preceded Rebecca's. Jane would never forget the visceral wail of despair as Mrs Robertson realised her daughter's death may have been preventable.

"I will not impose on you for long at this difficult time," Jane said, aware of everyone's eyes on her. "I know you have no reason to trust me, to believe that I can do anything to find Rebecca's killer, but I hope you will not object to me making some enquiries."

"Without your intervention, Miss Austen, we would not even be aware that Rebecca was murdered," Mrs Robertson said quietly. "I hold you to no promise, but I am grateful if there is something you can do to help us."

Jane inclined her head. "I need to ask you some questions. I mean no offence with any of them, and I make no assumptions about Rebecca. Sometimes it can be a little uncomfortable, but I promise you I do not ask anything to intentionally cause you pain." Jane waited to see if there was any objection then pushed on. "Francesca, you mentioned that Rebecca went out on the night of her death to meet a gentleman. What else can you tell me?"

"I hadn't known about it for long, perhaps three or four weeks, but I think she had been seeing him for longer," Francesca said. Jane noticed her clasp her hands together to stop them from shaking. "I begged her to tell me who it was she was meeting. I thought it terribly romantic."

"She never told you who the man was?"

Francesca shook her head. "I got the impression he was wealthy, or at least had some form of income. Rebecca said that one day they would travel the world together."

Jane nodded. Rebecca had been a young woman of marriageable age, from a respectable working family. There would be no reason to hide a courtship with a man from a similar background. There were a few possibilities for why a relationship would be kept secret: it was possible that Rebecca's gentleman was married, or that he was from a different social class.

"Anything else, Francesca?"

The young girl paused and then nodded. "She told me she was going to press him to reveal their relationship."

Jane digested this information. Rebecca had been going to press him. It meant the reluctance for their relationship to be public was on his part.

"Do you think I may see Rebecca's room?"

"She shared a room with Francesca," Mrs Robertson said. "I will take you up there."

"Thank you. Before you do, I wonder if you know anything about the other two young women Sir Phillip told us about?"

"Eliza Drayson," Mrs Robertson said quickly. "She was the lass found about six weeks ago. She was the same age as my Rebecca. Her parents run the inn in town. Eliza worked there."

"Did your daughter know her?"

"A little, but Rebecca's friends were mainly those that she went to school with. Rebecca and Eliza knew one another, but I do not think they were friends." Mrs Robertson chose her words carefully, but Jane realised the older woman did not think Eliza Drayson was the right sort of company for her daughter.

"My mother is being discreet," Captain Robertson said with a sad smile. "Eliza Drayson was unmarried and had had two children in the last three years. I do not wish to cast aspersions on her character, but Rebecca would not have socialised with her. She would not have risked her own reputation."

"How about the other young woman, the one found on the beach some months ago?"

"I remember them finding her body, of course. It was such a shock," Mrs Robertson said. "I did not know her, though, and I do not think Rebecca did either. She was the daughter of a fisherman and his wife in Charmouth. Their only daughter. I think they moved away after her death."

"Thank you," Jane said, making a note of the name and the details Mrs Robertson had been able to supply. It wasn't much to get started with. At first glance, there did not seem to be much to connect the three women, other than that they were all local, young and unmarried.

"I'll take you upstairs," Mrs Robertson said, pushing her chair back from the table.

The staircase led up to a small, square landing with four doors leading off. Mrs Robertson indicated the first room on the left and Jane went in, pausing in the doorway. She was struck by how like her own bedroom in Steventon it was. There was a small writing desk in the corner of the room and a double bed covered with a lovingly embroidered blanket. A heavy chest was at the end of the bed and on the window seat there were some cushions.

"She liked to sit and look out at the garden," Francesca said as she followed Jane into the room. "She could sit there for hours, lost in her thoughts."

"Have you always shared a room?"

"Always," Francesca said and Jane saw the glint of tears in the young girl's eyes. She thought of her close relationship with Cassandra and felt her pain. She could not imagine losing her beloved sister.

"May I?" Jane motioned towards the little writing desk and after receiving a nod of assent from Francesca began to carefully rifle through. It was neatly kept, paper and envelopes in a little draw and the inkpot and pens lined up, ready for use. There was no pile of correspondence waiting to be answered, no precious bundle of letters held together by ribbon, and Jane got the impression neither Francesca nor Rebecca were avid letter writers.

She stepped away and looked around the room, wondering where any precious keepsakes might be hidden. It was hard to keep secrets from someone you shared a room with, but Rebecca had successfully hidden the identity of her gentleman from her younger sister. Perhaps there had been other things she had hidden too.

"Which side of the bed was Rebecca's?" Jane asked.

"The left."

Jane perched on the edge of the bed and ran her hands over the blanket then down to check under the mattress. She had hoped she might find a letter or a love token tucked between the bed and mattress, but her hands came back empty. Next she searched the wooden chest, but there was nothing stashed away between the layers of clothes.

Jane stood in the middle of the room, almost ready to give up, and then her eyes alighted on the cushions by the window.

"Your sister liked to sit here?"

"Yes, sometimes for hours on end, looking out the window at the garden."

Approaching the window, Jane sat on the wide ledge. She looked out over the garden and then picked up one of the pillows. It was beautifully embroidered, the stitchwork precise and colourful.

"Did your sister embroider these?"

"No, our mother did."

"She is very accomplished."

"She tried to teach me and Rebecca, but we do not have her patience."

Jane picked one up and then another, her fingers probing the cushions. It was the final pillow that she paused over, wondering if there was a hint of stiffness that might signify something had been hidden inside. Carefully she untucked the covering and pressed her hand into the cushion. Her fingers closed around a slim package of papers.

"Have you found something?"

"I think so." Jane slowly withdrew the papers. There were three pieces, each folded a few times, the paper thick and of good quality, better than she could afford for her writing at home. With a glance at Francesca, she unfolded the first piece of paper, expecting to see a letter set out on the page. Instead there was a beautiful pencil drawing, full of detail and capturing the essence of Rebecca Robertson perfectly.

Jane felt a movement and glanced round to see Francesca at her shoulder, her eyes brimming with tears.

"It looks exactly like her," Francesca said softly.

Jane studied the picture. It was drawn completely in pencil, firmer and softer strokes creating the different shades that built to make an almost life-like picture of Rebecca. The young woman was shown smiling, her eyes cast down, a demure but alluring pose.

Turning the piece of paper over, Jane looked for a signature, knowing many artists signed their work even if it was just a rough sketch, but there was nothing.

Handing the picture to Francesca, she unfolded the second piece of paper. Again it was a drawing, this time of Rebecca lying back with her eyes closed. It was another excellent likeness, and Jane had the sense the artist had known Rebecca well. The third picture was a close-up sketch of two hands entwined, the fingers clasped together. From the drawing Jane could see one hand was smaller, more delicate, the other larger and masculine. She studied it for any details, but with a sigh acknowledged she was unlikely to identify the man from just a drawing of his hand.

"These are beautiful," Francesca said. "Do you think..." She trailed off.

Jane knew what she was thinking. It was hard to imagine that someone who had so lovingly captured the details of this young woman could then have murdered her.

"Do you have any idea who drew these, Francesca?"

"No."

Jane folded the pieces of paper up again and moved towards the door of the bedroom. She did not think there was anything more to be found in here.

Downstairs she showed the pictures to Captain Robertson and his mother, her heart sinking as they both shook their heads, not knowing who could have drawn them.

Mrs Robertson studied the picture of her daughter's face closely. "How could someone who can produce something so beautiful hurt my daughter?" she whispered, as tears streamed down her cheeks.

"We do not know this was drawn by the man who killed Rebecca," Jane said, placing a gentle hand on Mrs Robertson's shoulder.

"If only she had told me, trusted me. If only she had confided the identity of this man," Mrs Robertson said.

"You cannot blame yourself, Mother," Captain Robertson said quickly, his voice firm.

"What happens next, Miss Austen?" Mrs Robertson said. "What do we do?"

"Soon your daughter's body will arrive from the undertaker. You dress her and mourn her and arrange her funeral. In the years to come, it will be important for you to know you laid her to rest properly," Jane said, feeling a sudden rush of sadness that this woman would have to watch as her daughter was buried. "I need to reassure my family that I am well and tell my sister Cassandra all that has passed. Then, with your blessing, I would like to ask some questions of the people Rebecca knew to see if we can work out who her mystery gentleman was."

"You would do that?" Mrs Robertson asked, her expression a mixture of pain and hope.

"If you permit me. I have some experience in these matters."

"I do not wish for you to get into trouble with anyone — the officials here, or your parents."

Jane gave a grim smile. "I will be careful, Mrs Robertson, and I thank you for your concern."

Captain Robertson turned to Jane. "I will help you. The people of Lyme Regis are generally friendly, but they are more likely to talk to you if I am there."

"Thank you, Captain."

"Where do we start, Miss Austen?"

"With Rebecca's friends. Perhaps she confided in someone. Then I think we should speak to Eliza Drayson's family."

"Very well. Would you like me to walk you back to your rooms?"

"No, thank you, Captain. You stay with your mother. I think it is important you are here when your sister's body arrives."

Captain Robertson inclined his head and Jane took her leave, stepping out into the sunshine with a determined air.

CHAPTER EIGHT

"Jane Austen, where have you been? I have been out of my mind with worry." Mrs Austen drew Jane into an embrace as soon as she walked through the door. It was a little after two o'clock in the afternoon, and Jane had to concede she had been out a long time. It was hours since she had bid her parents and Cassandra farewell that morning to walk over the cliffs to Charmouth with Captain Robertson, and Jane felt a pang of guilt.

"What happened?" Cassandra said, gently urging Jane to sit in one of the comfortable armchairs.

She related the events of the morning, from the discoveries at the undertaker's to the confrontation with the coroner and magistrate at Mr Margill's home, and then her promise to Mrs Robertson to help find Rebecca's killer.

"You should not have promised that, Jane," Mrs Austen said.

Jane smiled reassuringly at her mother, knowing that after a while she would come round. Every time Jane set off to assist Lord Hinchbrooke with an investigation, Mrs Austen would voice her misgivings and let her wish that Jane would find a more suitable way to occupy her time be known, yet she had never actually stopped her from going. It was a delicate situation. Jane was an adult, yet still dependent in so many ways on her parents. She had no income of her own, no way of supporting herself. Some parents would use that as a way to manipulate their offspring into doing what they thought was best. Jane knew how fortunate she was that her parents allowed her the freedom to make her own decisions. In return, she did not dismiss their concerns.

"Captain Robertson is keen to be involved, Mama," Jane said. "I thought I would allow him to lead and I'll be more in the background, guiding him."

Cassandra shook her head. Thankfully she was behind Mrs Austen, so their mother did not see Cassandra's expression of disbelief. Jane letting Captain Robertson lead the investigation was as likely as a horse taking to the sky.

"We should return home to Steventon. Leave the locals to sort this out," Mrs Austen said, appealing to her husband.

Mr Austen let out a long-suffering sigh. "We have been blessed with two highly intelligent and capable daughters, my dear. Of course I would feel easier if they were safe at home, doing their needlework in front of the fire, but they would never be happy that way."

"You place their happiness over their safety?"

"I rate them both equally," Mr Austen said in a placating tone. Jane felt a swell of affection for her father. He was far from the domineering, patriarchal figure that ruled over many households. His decisions were always fair and balanced, and he had a unique insight into the motivations and desires of everyone around him. "I think it better this way. We will remain in Lyme Regis to ensure there is no danger."

"I dread to think what this could do to your reputations, girls," Mrs Austen said, collapsing into her chair.

"Our reputations will be just fine, Mama. Cassandra and I will ensure we are together at all times and Captain Robertson will provide some security."

"This man, this murderer you seek — he is killing young women, Jane," Mrs Austen said, her voice low.

Jane suddenly realised the fear her mother must be feeling. This was more than the routine protest she made each time

Jane announced she was embroiled in some new matter with Lord Hinchbrooke.

She reached across for her mother's hand. "Please believe me, Mama, when I say I do not underestimate the danger involved here. I think the same man, whoever he is, has killed three young women and he may go on to kill more unless someone stops him." She paused, glancing over at Cassandra. Her sister needed to know the extent of the risk they were taking. "The magistrate and the coroner, the men who should by now have found the culprit, have done nothing but hide the truth. I do not think that I alone can solve this crime, but I do think there is a chance that Cassandra and I, along with Captain Robertson, might be able to identify the murderer and stop him before he kills again."

Mrs Austen leaned forward in her chair and gripped Jane's hand. "I know you have the best of intentions, Jane. I have never questioned that. But you are placing yourself in danger, and the idea of losing you is too much to bear."

For a moment Jane sat in silence, contemplating her mother's words. It was hard to describe what propelled her to want to get involved in such a harrowing matter as this. She had a strong sense of justice, of wanting to see right done by the victim's family, but she also acknowledged there was something else, something less altruistic. Jane found people fascinating, how they treated one another, how they interacted. It was one of the reasons she was compelled to write, to instil the characters in her books with her observations on human nature. She could never go into the navy or the militia like her brothers Frank and Charles; she would never inherit a grand estate like Edward. She would never be allowed to attend university or take up a position in the clergy. Her mind was every bit as good as her brothers', and yet she was destined to be left behind. *This* was something she was carving out for herself, something that none of her brothers had done before her. It was hers and hers alone.

"I understand," Jane said to her mother. "I do not want to cause you unnecessary worry. Perhaps we can evaluate every day whether it would be prudent to return home."

It was a suggestion she knew her mother would like, though she fervently hoped that Mrs Austen would not insist they return to Steventon.

"Very well, Jane," Mrs Austen said wearily. "Please do not do anything to put yourself in the path of danger, and think at least a little upon your reputation. It is not all that far from Lyme Regis to Hampshire, and gossip spreads fast."

Jane inclined her head and then rose from her chair, eager to eat something and then head out into Lyme Regis to find out what she could about Rebecca Robertson from her friends.

Jane and Cassandra walked arm in arm through the streets of the little town, heads bent to shade their faces from the sun. It was another hot day, the afternoon sky a brilliant blue with not a single cloud to cool the temperature. Jane had the ribbons of her bonnet undone and hanging loose over her shoulders — the bow irritated her chin, and as there was no breeze today, the chances of losing her bonnet in a gust of wind were low.

For Jane it was reassuring to have Cassandra back by her side. Just a few years earlier she would have done her best to shield her sister from recent events, but Cassandra had slowly come to accept Jane's fascination with crime and was now her staunchest ally.

"I cannot believe anyone could do such a thing," Cassandra said. "Three deaths. It is not as though any of the murders were committed in the heat of passion, or in panic."

"Indeed," Jane said. "The man we hunt is calculating. He has planned things meticulously." She paused as a thought struck her. "I wonder if he always planned to kill Miss Robertson? That could be why he urged her to keep their relationship a secret. Or perhaps he was concerned about people finding out for another reason?"

Cassandra looked horrified. "Imagine the sort of man who would start a relationship with a woman, purely with the intention of killing her at some point."

"It would be like nothing we have seen before."

They paused outside the Horn Tavern, looking up at the white painted façade and the sign swinging over the door. It looked tatty, the paint peeling around the windows and the glass itself grimy and streaked with dirt. Jane was aware how difficult it was to keep any building looking neat so close to the sea, with the relentless wind and salt spray always chipping away at the paint and softening the wood around the windows, yet the Horn Tavern seemed more neglected than its neighbours.

"This is where Eliza Drayson lived?" Cassandra asked, peering up at the building and wrinkling her nose.

"Yes, she lived here with her parents and worked in the inn." Jane lowered her voice discreetly, aware of the other people in the street. "Captain Robertson told me she had two babies in the past three years outside of wedlock."

There were a number of possible explanations. Eliza Drayson may have had a lover and been unlucky or unknowledgeable about the methods some women used to try to reduce their chance of getting pregnant. There were any number of reasons a lover might not have been able to marry her; he may have been married already or unsuitable in some other way. Of course, there was also the more unsavoury possibility that Eliza had received payment for providing services of an intimate nature to the inn's patrons. It was common practice in some of the less salubrious establishments, especially in the towns and cities, and it might explain why Mrs Robertson did not think Eliza Drayson was suitable company for her daughter.

Jane pushed open the door, wondering if the Draysons would talk to them without a formal introduction. If they were suspicious of strangers, she would have to return later with Captain Robertson, yet she hoped to conduct this interview with just Cassandra with her.

There were four customers in the dingy inn, all sitting alone, nursing their drinks in the gloom. There was no friendly discussion between them, no acknowledgement that they knew anyone else was in the room. Forcing herself inside, Jane walked briskly over to the counter. She had been in plenty of inns before, but not many like this. Normally they were respectable establishments for weary travellers. She would have a bedchamber and take her meal in the dining room, but never enter the main room.

With more confidence than she felt, Jane addressed the man behind the counter. He was in his forties, short and rotund. He didn't look up at their approach, but instead continued to rub at the counter with a dirty cloth.

"I am looking for Mr and Mrs Drayson," Jane said, speaking clearly but quietly, not wanting the whole of Lyme Regis to know their business.

"Who is asking?" the man replied, his words slurring into one another. Jane regarded him a little closer. He had on a thick apron over shirtsleeves, rolled up to reveal once powerful arms that had gone to fat. There was a spider's web of veins across his nose and cheeks, and one side of his mouth drooped a little at the edge, not moving when he spoke.

"My name is Miss Jane Austen and this is my sister, Miss Cassandra Austen. We wish to talk to Mr and Mrs Drayson about their daughter Eliza."

The man regarded them with an inscrutable expression for a few seconds and then pushed himself up onto his feet, shuffling along the bar to a door at the end.

"Ann, someone here about Eliza," the man shouted, not waiting for a reply before limping back to his spot.

No one appeared for a few minutes, and Jane was beginning to feel uncomfortable when a woman about the same age as the man appeared in the doorway he had shouted through. She glared at Jane and Cassandra, looking round the room before slowly making her way over.

"What do you want?"

Jane repeated the introductions and asked if they could go somewhere more private. Mrs Drayson looked as though she might refuse but then motioned for them to follow her upstairs.

The private rooms of the inn were even less appealing than the public ones, and Jane felt a deep revulsion set in as they were shown into a filthy room that seemed to act as both bedchamber and sitting room.

"Sit down if you must," Mrs Drayson said, pushing a pile of scraps of fabric to one side to make space for her to sit on one of the chairs. Jane and Cassandra perched on the small sofa, facing her. "Eliza is dead."

"You have our condolences," Jane said softly. "You are her mother, Mrs Drayson?"

"Yes."

"Is your husband around? It might be helpful if we speak to both of you."

Mrs Drayson let out a bark of laughter. "You met him, downstairs. He won't be any use to you."

"Is Mr Drayson unwell?"

"His brain has been addled by drink and he lost what little sense he had left a few months ago. Apoplexy."

It explained the slurred speech and the drooping of his face. Jane nodded sympathetically.

"Useless lump can just about drag a barrel around now."

"I am sorry," Cassandra said, giving Mrs Drayson a tentative smile.

"Nothing for you to be sorry about. The useless old maggot did this to himself."

"We wanted to talk to you about Eliza," Jane said, realising they were not going to persuade Mrs Drayson to call her husband upstairs. "I do not know if you had heard, but another young woman — Rebecca Robertson — was found dead on the beach yesterday."

"Yes, everyone is saying she fell from the cliffs."

Jane cleared her throat. She knew she could not openly contradict the story the magistrate and coroner had circulated, but she had to somehow make people aware that the deaths were connected.

"Eliza was found on the beach as well, I am told, and another young woman a few months before Eliza."

Mrs Drayson frowned, her eyes flicking from Jane to Cassandra and back again. "Eliza drowned."

Jane didn't say anything for a moment, allowing the silence to stretch out and cast some doubt in Mrs Drayson's mind.

"There was an inquest. They said she drowned."

"Sometimes the inquests do not get everything right," Jane said softly. "Three young women have been found dead on the same beach within the last five months."

"What are you saying? Someone killed my Eliza?"

"I believe so, Mrs Drayson."

Mrs Drayson's face twisted in pain and disbelief. "Who killed her?"

"I do not know. I was hoping you might be able to help us get a clearer picture of Eliza's life in her last few months."

"What do you want to know?"

"Anything. What was she like? What did she enjoy doing? Who were her friends? How did she spend her time?"

Mrs Drayson shrugged her shoulders. "She worked, she went out. She was twenty years old — I hardly kept her under lock and key."

"She worked here, in the inn?"

"Yes, she served the customers. We've been here for ten years, so she grew up washing pots and clearing tables."

"How about friends? Who did she spend her time with?"

Mrs Drayson shrugged again. "I didn't question Eliza every time she went out."

Jane and Cassandra waited expectantly.

Mrs Drayson sighed. "Mabel Nielson — she lives in one of the cottages along the front now with her husband, but she was friends with Eliza."

"Was there a gentleman? Someone your daughter was courting?"

The older woman looked away, her eyes dancing around the room for a moment. "Not anyone in particular."

Jane paused, wondering if Eliza's mother was keeping something from them. And if so, why?

Clearing her throat, Jane pressed on with the difficult question. "We heard Eliza had been with child in the last few years…"

"It is hardly a secret. She got pregnant. Twice. The first child died when it was four days old, a sickly creature from the start."

"And the second?"

"That one survived. Eliza found some woman in Sidmouth that wanted a baby and gave him to her."

"She did not want to keep the baby?"

Mrs Drayson gave a mirthless laugh. "And support him with what? Eliza was unwed, already judged by everyone in this town. People would turn away from her in the street, whisper about her behind their hands."

"That must have been very difficult for her," Cassandra said gently. "And for you."

"What did she care what it did to me? Eliza never thought of anyone other than herself."

"What about the baby's father? Was he still around?"

Mrs Drayson shrugged, seeming not to know or care.

"Do you have any idea who could have killed your daughter, Mrs Drayson?"

"No." She hesitated and then shook her head firmly. "If she was murdered, I don't know who could have done it."

Jane stood. "I wonder if I might see Eliza's room, or any of her personal possessions?"

"Her room's gone," Mrs Drayson said quickly. "We had to turn it into a bedroom for paying customers. And the little Eliza had, we burned once she was buried."

It was a strange thing to do and Jane frowned. Something didn't feel right. Mrs Drayson had not reacted to the news of her daughter's murder as Jane would expect, and she wondered if the older woman had something to hide.

"I see. Well, thank you for your help, Mrs Drayson," Jane said as they made their way to the door and the stairs beyond.

"Perhaps we can return in a few days to see if you have thought of anything relevant," Cassandra added.

"Perhaps," Mrs Drayson muttered. She escorted them all the way to the door and out onto the street, her eyes boring into them as they walked away. Jane did not speak until they had rounded a corner and were free from her stare.

"That was strange, was it not?" Jane said as she linked her arm through Cassandra's.

"Indeed. I kept thinking how our mother would react if she was informed one of us had been murdered. Mrs Drayson's reaction was so far from what I could imagine — almost as if she already knew."

"I do not think she knew," Jane said slowly, trying to work out what had felt so wrong in the upstairs rooms of the Horn Tavern. "I think she was genuinely surprised at the suggestion Eliza was murdered, but it was as though she couldn't bring herself to care."

"And the way she hurried us out at the end — that was very odd."

"I had planned to call at the Robertsons' house to ask Captain Robertson to accompany us to see Rebecca's friends, but I wonder if we should go to see Mabel Nielson first. Perhaps she can shed some light on what sort of person Eliza was and who she spent her time with."

"Good idea."

They walked quickly through the streets until they came out by the Cobb, asking a woman out with her children for directions to Mabel Nielson's house.

In contrast to the Horn Tavern, the little cottage on the seafront was immaculately kept. Small in size, it looked freshly painted and the brass doorknocker shone as if it had been polished only moments before.

Jane knocked on the door, wondering at the presence of a heavy brass doorknocker on an otherwise unassuming little cottage.

A young woman opened the door. She was plump and pretty with a smattering of freckles over her nose. Her hair was pulled back and covered with a cotton mob cap. She had a baby in her arms and a small child clinging to one leg.

"Good afternoon," Jane said with a smile. "We are looking for Mabel Nielson."

"I am Mabel Nielson." The young woman suddenly frowned. "Has something happened to my Albert?"

"Albert is your husband?"

"Yes."

Jane shook her head. "No, we are here to talk to you about Eliza Drayson."

Mabel visibly relaxed before frowning again. "Poor Eliza. Excuse me, my husband Albert works on the boats in the morning, and then when money is tight he does some labouring work for Lord Willingham on his estate. Ever since I've had the babes I worry so much, always thinking the worst has happened."

"I am sorry we gave you cause for concern, Mrs Nielson."

"Would you like to come in? I haven't got much to offer you, but there is tea on the stove and I have some fruit cake from earlier in the week."

"That is very kind," Jane said, stepping inside as Mabel led the way. She shifted the baby into her other arm and ushered the young child along the passage in front of her.

The cottage was tiny, just two small rooms downstairs, the largest of which was the kitchen. There were some stools around a table and a comfortable rocking chair set in front of the unlit fire. Another child, this one about three years old, was playing with a roughly carved wooden horse on the floor.

"Please do not trouble yourself," Jane said as Mabel began fussing around, fetching cups for the tea.

"It's no trouble." A minute later steaming cups of tea were set in front of them along with a small slice of cake, a few precious raisins dotted throughout. Jane was aware what a luxury this cake would be to this family, but it would be rude to refuse it even for the most altruistic of reasons, and she got the sense Mabel enjoyed being hostess with what little she had to share. "You said you wanted to talk of Eliza?"

"Yes, I understand you were friends with her."

Mabel puffed out her cheeks and settled into the rocking chair, soothing the baby as it stirred in her arms. "We were friends. Although we were not as close as we once had been." Mabel motioned towards her children playing on the floor. "I became preoccupied with the babies, and Albert, my husband, did not like me mixing with Eliza, so we grew apart. Our lives were very different."

"We have just come from speaking to Mrs Drayson," Jane said, warming to the young woman in front of her. She seemed genuine and honest. "I expect you have heard Rebecca Robertson was found dead on the beach yesterday morning."

"Yes, poor Rebecca. I knew her too, although not as well as Eliza. They said Eliza's death was an accident, Rebecca's too."

"I am not convinced that is the case. I think someone killed them both, and another young woman from Charmouth, who was found on the beach a few months before Eliza."

Mabel's hand flew to her mouth and she let out a small cry. "Someone killed them?"

Jane nodded. "I believe so. Rebecca's family have been very helpful in building a picture of who she was and who she had contact with, but we are struggling to find out much about Eliza. I hoped you might be able to help us."

"I don't expect her mother was very helpful," Mabel said, the words barely more than a whisper.

"Why do you say that?"

Mabel sighed and shook her head. "I should not be so uncharitable. She lost her daughter, after all. But Mrs Drayson was not ever kind to Eliza — she was not ever kind to anyone."

"Can you tell us about Eliza?"

For a long moment Mabel didn't speak, instead looking down at the baby in her arms with a faraway expression.

"I'd known Eliza since I was ten years old. Her parents moved to Lyme Regis ten years ago and took over the Horn Tavern. They lived above the inn. I think they were from somewhere in Sussex before then, but Eliza didn't really talk about it." Mabel smiled as she remembered happier times. "She was a whirlwind, always getting into mischief. She would run along the Cobb when a storm was coming in, laughing as the seawater splashed over her. She could have been swept out to sea, but it was as if she didn't care. Eliza would always do the dangerous thing, whatever we had been warned against."

"Did you attend school?"

"For a year. There is a school in Lyme Regis and we all went together for a short while, Eliza and Rebecca and me. Eliza's mum pulled her out first, saying she needed Eliza to work at the inn. I stayed for another year, Rebecca a little less, I think.

Rebecca went to Miss Warkworth's school for a time as well, but that was later on."

Jane nodded. It was interesting Eliza and Rebecca had been at school together, although not unexpected in a small place like Lyme Regis.

"Eliza worked at the inn after that. She hated it. Hated the smell and the customers, hated being ordered around by her parents all the time."

Jane thought back to the filthy tavern and could understand a young girl's reluctance to spend all her time in the dank and dingy environment.

Mabel shrugged. "That was her life. We would go for walks on the beach together, talk about the boys we liked. There isn't exactly much to do around here. Eliza always said she wanted to leave, but she knew no one outside of Lyme Regis. She had nowhere else to go."

"We know Eliza had two children," Cassandra said, her voice full of empathy.

"Yes." Mabel looked down for a moment. "You've seen the inn; it isn't exactly thriving and things were even worse a few years ago. Mrs Drayson encouraged Eliza to take some of the customers up on their offer to pay her if she took them upstairs."

"Her mother encouraged that?"

"Her mother arranged it. Eliza hated it, hated her mother, and hated the men."

"It became a regular thing?"

"No, not all the time, just when they were particularly short of money. Then Eliza got pregnant. She was seventeen." Mabel motioned towards the eldest of her children playing on the floor. "I was married by then and pregnant with Polly. As you can see, we're not wealthy, but, because I was married, my pregnancies were all seen as the blessings they are. Eliza's made her an outcast."

"People can be cruel."

"She stopped going out. She said she couldn't deal with the way everyone looked at her and whispered. Yet she hated being at the inn, taunted by her mother and ignored by her father. When she gave birth I went to see her and the baby, a beautiful little boy. He was sickly from the start and didn't live past four days old." Mabel sighed and held her baby closer to her. "She said it was for the best, that death was better than growing up knowing you were a bastard, but I could see she was devastated."

"It must have been an awful time for her."

Mabel nodded.

"Then she got pregnant again," Jane prompted.

"Yes, although that was different. She had been in a deep melancholy, and each week I thought I might hear the news that she had done something terrible." Mabel gave Jane a meaningful look and Jane inclined her head to show she understood the young woman was talking about suicide. "I didn't really see her for months and then she showed up pregnant, this time happy and hopeful for the future."

"Did she tell you who the father was?"

"No, she wouldn't. I asked, of course, thinking perhaps her mother had pressed her to start selling herself again, but Eliza said that she had a man who would look after her, provide for her and the baby."

"Did she talk of marriage?"

Mabel shook her head. "No, but I got the impression she thought that was where it would lead. She became melancholy again whilst she was pregnant, and I assumed her man had backed away with the prospect of fatherhood looming, then, suddenly, she was all happy again."

"I gather she didn't keep the baby after he was born?" Jane said, wondering if this was when Eliza had realised the promises her lover had made to her were empty.

"She said the baby had been placed with a childless couple in Sidmouth. I thought she would be devastated, but when I asked her about it she just shrugged and said everything would work out for the best." Mabel paused to drop a kiss on her child's head. "Eliza died about two months after the baby was born."

"I hadn't realised it was so soon after the birth."

They all fell silent, contemplating how difficult Eliza's life had been.

"I didn't really see her much before she died. She was preoccupied, and I had the children to look after. I didn't press the matter. Albert is a good man and a kind husband, but Eliza had a notorious reputation and he preferred it if I didn't spend too much time with her."

"Did she ever tell you anything more about this man of hers?"

Mabel shook her head. "No, she was very secretive. All she said was that he had promised to take her away. She told me nothing of his background. At first I thought perhaps he was a visitor to the town — we have a number of people come here on holiday now or to take the sea air — but later I wondered if she had been so secretive because he was a local. A married man, maybe, or someone who did not want to be publicly associated with Eliza."

Jane nodded, again wondering if the reason for the secrecy may have been because he had always planned to end the relationship by strangling Eliza and leaving her body on the beach.

"Thank you, Mrs Nielson," Jane said. "You have been very helpful. I now have a much clearer picture of Eliza and her life."

"I am glad you care enough to ask. All her life she has been an afterthought."

Jane mused on how this was true. Even in death Eliza's demise had not been enough to trigger a full investigation. It was only with Rebecca Robertson's murder that hers had even been noticed.

"We will not take up any more of your time, but if you think of anything else please do contact us. We are staying at Mrs Riley's."

"I wish you luck," Mabel said, rising to her feet. The baby in her arms let out a little squawk at the movement, but soon settled as Mabel rocked from side to side.

They made their way out of the kitchen and were almost at the door when it opened and a tall man walked through, stopping in surprise when he saw Jane and Cassandra in the hallway.

"Good afternoon," he said, a frown upon his face.

"Good afternoon," Jane said, taking in the young man's handsome face and tanned skin.

"Albert," Mabel said, a smile spreading across her face. "This is Miss Jane Austen and Miss Cassandra Austen. They came to talk to me about Eliza."

The young man looked suddenly wary. "Mabel knew her from when they were children, nothing more," he said sharply.

"Hush, Albert, they are not here to rake over Eliza's reputation, or try to blacken mine by association." Mabel turned to Jane and Cassandra. "He is protective of me." She returned her focus to her husband. "They think Eliza was murdered, along with Rebeca Robertson, and were asking me what I knew of her."

"Murdered? I heard the verdict at the inquest was accidental death."

Jane cleared her throat. "The magistrate and coroner will be investigating further, but they did not want to spread panic in the town. Did you know Eliza Drayson, Mr Nielson?"

He shrugged, moving past them in the narrow hallway and heading towards the kitchen. "As much as anyone in this town. I knew *of* her, would raise my cap in greeting if we came face to face, but I did not know her. She had a bad reputation and I told Mabel to keep her distance."

It was clear Albert Nielson had no more to say on the matter as he disappeared into the kitchen. As Jane and Cassandra moved out of the front door, Jane glanced back to see the young man sitting in the rocking chair and kicking off his boots, a frown on his face.

Jane turned to leave when Mabel reached out and took her hand.

"Thank you for not forgetting Eliza. It is easy for people to try to brush her memory away. She made them uncomfortable, I think; they saw how a pleasant young girl could fall so far so quickly. But her life was no less valuable than any other."

Jane nodded in agreement and as she and Cassandra walked away, she felt Mabel's eyes on them until they rounded the corner.

CHAPTER NINE

Cassandra looped her arm through Jane's, and for a long time they walked in silence before finding themselves on the damp sands of the beach. The tide was a long way out, but on the turn, and a great expanse of sand stretched before them.

"Poor girl," Cassandra said eventually.

"Indeed. At least we now know what it was her mother was hiding from us."

Cassandra nodded, her expression glum. "I know there are terrible people in this world, Jane, and others are forced to do terrible things in order to survive. It is easy for me to stand here in my position of comfort and judge the actions of others, but what mother would push her daughter into selling herself? It is unthinkable. Eliza would have been sixteen at most."

Jane thought again what a sad life Eliza had led. Used and abused by those around her and finally, when she thought she had found some happiness, some hope of a future, someone had snuffed out her life.

"There is a pattern here," Jane said as they walked along the sand. There were other people on the beach, but too far away to hear their conversation, so she spoke freely. "Both Rebecca and Eliza hid their courtship from their friends and families, perhaps on the urging of the man they were seeing. Both spoke of their hopes for a better life. For Eliza that meant getting away from Lyme Regis; for Rebecca it meant travelling the world."

"Surely it cannot be a coincidence," Cassandra said.

"Lord Hinchbrooke always reminds me not to narrow my focus too early on in an investigation. I think it is important to remember that these young women had many acquaintances in common."

Cassandra nodded. "I suppose there is the chance that Rebecca went out to meet her gentleman two nights ago, but he was not the person who killed her. Someone else could have attacked her, either before or after he arrived."

"Perhaps," Jane said, although she was not convinced. Surely if the man courting Rebecca were innocent, he would have come forward by now to tell what he knew and to clear his name.

They had turned towards the sea, walking across the sand until they had to stop lest their hems become sodden with seawater.

"How are we going to find him, Jane?"

Jane stared out at the sea while she gathered her thoughts. "There are not all that many men in Lyme Regis. As we get to know each of the victims a little better, as we dig into their worlds, we will find them. Assuming that both Eliza and Rebecca were killed by the same man, they must have crossed paths with him at some point."

Cassandra shuddered. "You would think we would be able to recognise such a predatory soul, were we to come across him, but if he has fooled three women already, I doubt it will be obvious."

Jane nodded thoughtfully, reminded by Cassandra's comment of the first young woman who had been found dead five months earlier. As yet they did not even know her name. "If the same man was courting the first victim when she died, then he must also have been courting Eliza at the same time, if he was the father of her second child."

"Yes," Cassandra said thoughtfully. "If he was the father, it speaks of a long entanglement. At least ten or eleven months, but perhaps more than a year."

"How can someone get that close to another, share so much with them, promise them the world, then take their life as if they meant nothing?"

Cassandra reached out and took Jane's hand. "You will find this man, Jane. You will find him, and then he will pay for his crimes."

Jane felt the weight of responsibility press down on her. Of course she was not alone: Captain Robertson would not rest until his sister's killer was found and, despite their actions to cover up the murders, Jane thought Mr Margill and Sir Phillip would also be hunting the murderer. Yet she had stepped up to this task, had decided to make it her mission to find the person who had so cruelly taken three women's lives, and as such she could not rest until they were in custody, awaiting trial for the murders.

"I will find him," Jane said. "I will find this murderer."

Cassandra gave Jane's hand a squeeze. "So, where next?"

"Let us call upon the Robertsons and see if we can meet some of Rebecca's friends. I think it will be easier with an introduction from Captain Robertson."

They turned away from the sea and began the walk back up the beach. It only took a few minutes to walk through the town, and soon they were approaching the Robertsons' house. Outside was a beautiful carriage with a team of four horses standing to attention. The horses were black and sleek and looked as though they could give even the fastest racehorses a good race.

"That is quite a carriage," Jane murmured as they made their way around it and up to the front door. Before she could raise her hand to knock, the door opened and a tall, thin man who looked to be in his fifties bore down on her.

Jane took a step back. She would have stumbled had it not been for Cassandra's steadying hand on her arm.

The man paused when he saw Jane and Cassandra. There was an air of superiority about him, but after a moment he offered the hint of a smile.

"You must be Miss Jane Austen and Miss Cassandra Austen," he said, his accent confirming he was from the upper classes, with no hint of a Dorset drawl.

"We are," Jane said, inclining her head. "You have us at a disadvantage, sir. I do not think we have been introduced."

"Lord Willingham," he offered, affecting a half bow.

"Thank you ever so much for your visit, my lord," Mrs Robertson said, appearing behind his shoulder.

Lord Willingham turned and took her hand, holding it between his. "Anything I can do for you, please do not hesitate to ask." He turned back to Jane and Cassandra, casting them a curious look. "I understand you have offered to help the Robertsons in their quest to find out what happened to dear Rebecca."

"We have."

"Is this not something best left to the magistrate?"

"Of course," Jane said. "Yet sometimes it does not hurt to approach things from a different direction." She didn't doubt Lord Willingham knew of the attempted cover-up by the coroner and magistrate. Men of his status had connections everywhere and were always the first to know what was happening in their area. Many of the families in and around Lyme Regis would have someone who worked for Lord Willingham, and no doubt he was landlord to a fair number as well. Some members of the aristocracy sat behind their high gates and did not interest themselves in the affairs of their tenants and neighbours, but Jane got the impression Lord Willingham was a man who liked to involve himself in local concerns.

"This family is grieving, Miss Austen. I do hope you are not planning on taking advantage of them." It was an insult, especially so early on in their acquaintance, and for a moment Jane was stunned into silence. A few years ago she would have let her temper get the better of her and argued back. Now, she simply smiled sweetly, lifted her chin ever so slightly and held Lord Willingham's eye.

"They are grieving the loss of a daughter and a sister, an irreplaceable loss. It is something that will live within them forever. The situation needs to be dealt with delicately and with grace, yet the very men who are meant to protect us and deliver answers told them that Miss Robertson's death was an accident." She paused. "I have nothing to gain personally by helping the family, but it is the right thing to do, and I have been raised to do the right thing, no matter how difficult."

"I did not mean to cause offence, Miss Austen, but I too am invested in the welfare of this family. Sometimes even the most well-meaning amongst us can make a bad situation worse with our actions."

"I am not offended, Lord Willingham," Jane said, catching sight of Mrs Robertson's concerned expression over Lord Willingham's shoulder.

Lord Willingham gave a small nod and turned again to Mrs Robertson. "Send word if there is anything you need. My prayers are with you and your family."

"Thank you," Mrs Robertson said, giving a weak smile. "You have been so kind."

Lord Willingham strode away, hopping up into the carriage and banging on the ceiling to alert the driver he was ready to depart.

Jane and Cassandra watched the carriage until it rounded the corner and then turned back to the house. Captain Robertson was already stepping out of the door, leaning in to give his mother a kiss on the cheek.

"My mother is exhausted. Francesca is with a friend, so I thought we could go for a stroll to give my mother some time to herself. She bathed and dressed Rebecca's body earlier, with the help of some of our neighbours, and I think the task overwhelmed her a little."

Jane inclined her head, and together they made their way back to the street.

"It was good of Lord Willingham to call by and pay his respects," Jane said. "He still looks out for your family."

"He does. He has been most generous since my father died and even now, years on, he always spares us a thought when he has more than discharged his responsibility to the family of one of his late workers."

They walked in silence for a minute and then Jane pushed on, wanting to tell the young captain of their morning.

"Cassandra and I went to speak to Eliza Drayson's mother a little earlier today," Jane began, pausing when she saw Captain Robertson's expression.

"I doubt she was very helpful."

"No, she wasn't, but we also went to see Mrs Mabel Nielson. She was a friend of Eliza's, especially before she got married and had children. She told us a little about Eliza's life. It was a sad existence."

The captain nodded. "I remember when they were children. Rebecca and Eliza and Mabel would collect shells on the beach. They were all innocents. Yet Eliza's life turned out so different, so painful."

Jane glanced at Captain Robertson and took a gamble. "You knew her mother pressed her into selling herself for money?"

Captain Robertson grimaced and Jane realised he was a little prudish about such things, despite spending the last few years in the army.

"Poverty can do cruel things to people. Eliza was a sweet-looking girl, although she was always getting into trouble. Later, she changed. It was like she had become a different person. Life was not kind to her and nor were the people of this town."

They had reached the promenade and Jane was glad for the cooling sea breeze.

"Shall we walk out onto the Cobb?" Captain Robertson suggested. "I will tell you of Rebecca's friends and we can decide when we will pay them a visit."

They strolled onto the harbour wall, stepping around a group of small children who were sitting with their feet dangling over the side.

"Rebecca had two close friends, Miss Hettie Wright and Miss Lucy Ringwood. They both live in Charmouth and attended Miss Warkworth's School for Young Ladies."

"Your sister would walk over to visit them?"

"Yes, or if it was a fine day they might make plans to meet on the beach. As you no doubt have seen, much of our leisure time involves either a stroll on the cliffs or a walk on the beach here in Lyme Regis."

Jane glanced up at the sky. The sun was still bright but dropping quickly. It must have been approaching five o'clock, and she doubted there would be time to walk to Charmouth and back that evening.

"Rebecca's funeral will be held the day after tomorrow. I expect the news of her death has reached the Wrights and Ringwoods by now, but if we plan to go to Charmouth tomorrow I can let Rebecca's friends know about the funeral. I am sure they would want to attend."

Jane tempered down her frustration that it would be another day before she spoke to Rebecca's friends. It was the only sensible option; it would be highly foolish to walk along the cliffs in the dark. Rebecca's friends would wait until the morning, and it meant she could think on what she had learned so far.

"Tell me, Miss Austen, do you have any idea who killed Rebecca?" Captain Robertson said suddenly and then shook his head. "Forgive me, of course you do not. I grow impatient when I should be supportive."

"I do not blame you for your impatience, Captain. It would be unnatural if you were not keen for an answer, to allow justice to be done so your family can mourn in peace."

He sighed and looked out to sea. "I just wish…" He trailed off and Jane wondered how he would have finished that sentence. Perhaps he wished he had been home more to look after his sister. Perhaps he wished Rebecca hadn't been taken in by the false promises of a man who would go on to kill her. Or perhaps he wished the murderer had never set his sights on Rebecca.

Jane laid a comforting hand on his arm. "We will find the person who killed your sister," she said with a note of determination in her voice.

For a long time this tragedy would be the event that dominated his life. It would be the first thing he thought of in the morning and the last thing at night. What was more, it would be the thing that people identified him by. No longer would he be just Captain Robertson; he would be the man whose sister was murdered.

"Thank you, Miss Austen." He pulled himself up so he stood with a rigid, military posture. "I think I should return home, check on my mother. Miss Jane, Miss Cassandra, thank you for everything you have done today. I am most grateful."

He turned and strode off at such a pace that he had disappeared into the streets of Lyme Regis before they could bid him farewell.

CHAPTER TEN

The scene when Jane and Cassandra returned to their lodgings was not a happy one. Mr and Mrs Austen were sitting by the open window with expressions of concern on their faces. Another seat was filled, and Jane let out a quiet groan as she saw the wiry figure of Sir Phillip look up as they entered.

He gave a tight little smile that didn't reach his eyes. "Miss Jane Austen and Miss Cassandra Austen, we were wondering when you would return. You should have a care for your safety with a murderer on the loose." It was a comment meant to provoke a reaction, and to Jane's horror her mother responded just as the coroner would have wanted.

"It is not safe, girls. Sir Phillip here has told us of the gravity of the situation, of the danger this *man* —" she shuddered and had to compose herself before continuing —"this *murderer* poses to young women of your age. Three women are dead and who knows when he will strike again? The poor residents of Lyme Regis have to stay here, but we do not."

Jane felt her heart sink.

"How delightful to see you again, Sir Phillip," Cassandra said from over Jane's shoulder. As always, Cassandra was composed and polite and even managed to sound like she meant the kind words of greeting. "I did not know you would be calling on our parents."

"I felt it was my duty, Miss Austen. Alas, I have never been blessed with children, but if I had I would want someone to inform me if they were charging into a dangerous situation such as this without my full knowledge of exactly what they were getting into."

"So thoughtful," Cassandra said, without even a hint of irony in her voice.

"Now you are safely home, it is time for me to take my leave." Sir Phillip stood and bowed. "I wish you all an uneventful journey home."

Mr Austen showed him out, with no one saying a word until he returned.

"Mama —" Jane began when it was just the four of them.

Mrs Austen held up a hand and Jane fell silent, but it was her father who spoke.

"I am torn, girls. All your lives I have striven to give you opportunities that most young women do not have. I have tried not to stifle you, to encourage your passions and your creativity. I have spoken to you as equals, never subjected you to the belief that you cannot achieve greatness in this world because of your sex." He shook his head. "Even when you insisted on following Lord Hinchbrooke into danger, I suppressed the fatherly fear that blossomed inside me. Yet it has brought us to this."

Jane pressed her lips together, aware of the importance of this moment. Her father had always been lenient, and she desperately hoped he would not change his approach now.

"Jane, you are my high-flying swift, reaching extraordinary heights. I have always known you were destined for something great. And Cassandra, you are true and loyal and the kindest young woman in all of Hampshire. The good Lord knows I love all my children, and I want the opportunity to see what you make of your lives."

"Papa," Jane said, unable to stay silent any longer. "Sir Phillip is —"

"Manipulating us," her father interrupted, finishing Jane's sentence, and she was reminded that her father was an astute man. He was well educated — his degree from Oxford could attest to that — but he also understood human nature. That came from the years working as a rector, helping people to settle disputes, to come to terms with loss and disappointment. "I know exactly what Sir Phillip is trying to do, Jane. It riles me just as it riles you, yet it does not mean the man is incorrect. There *is* a killer stalking the streets of Lyme Regis, and if he realises you and Cassandra are on his trail, he may turn his attention to you." He paused, looking at them with fatherly love and affection. "What sort of father would I be if I did not seek to protect my daughters from such a man?"

"What about the greater good?" Jane said softly, knowing there was no point in raising her voice. Her father was a scholar and appreciated a well-reasoned argument above histrionics. "I can make a difference here. Sir Phillip doesn't care, nor does Mr Margill. If we return home now, another young woman might be seduced by this man and lose her life, and I could have perhaps prevented it."

"One day I pray you know the burden of having children, Jane," Mrs Austen said. Until now she had listened to the exchange silently. "It is the most incredible of blessings, but you have never known worry until you have a child to fret about."

Jane moved across the room and clasped her mother's hand. "I know you worry, Mama."

"I cannot help but worry. You charge into these situations without any thought for your own safety, Jane. Your life is not gilded; it is not like the lives of the women you write about in your stories. If some terrible accident befalls you, then there will be no miraculous recovery."

Mrs Austen's worry permeated the room. Mr Austen held up his hands and shook his head. "I expect this panic is what Sir Phillip wanted. Let us not make any hasty decisions this evening. Instead we will rest and consider our options and discuss things again in the morning."

It was the best outcome Jane could hope for, and as she and Cassandra excused themselves to get ready for dinner she breathed a sigh of relief. The short alliance between herself and the magistrate and coroner seemed to be over before it had really begun. She reasoned they must have decided it was safer to get her out of the picture altogether.

The next morning was overcast and dull, the sun obscured by thick clouds. There had been some rain overnight, pattering on the windows and keeping Jane awake. As was her custom, she had risen early. She had carefully removed the manuscript she was working on from the leather bindings that protected it whilst she was travelling and had spent a long time contemplating a near empty page. She had started this novel, entitled 'Lady Susan', a few weeks earlier as they had prepared for their summer trip to Lyme Regis. Jane loved starting a new book; the possibilities of what could happen were endless. Normally at this point she wrote in a fury, her tiny handwriting filling sheet after sheet of paper. It was only as the book progressed and she had to draw the threads of the story together that she slowed, going through and re-writing sections, editing as she developed the characters and crossing out the parts she didn't like.

Today she had written at most a few hundred words, each carefully chosen and dragged from her mind with great effort. In truth her heart was not in the story this morning. She stared at the paper and instead of beautifully formed words she saw only Rebecca Robertson's dead body, her eyes glassy and unseeing, the horrible bruising around her neck.

A few years ago she would have chastised herself for the little she had managed to achieve this morning, but recently she had started to acknowledge the emotional toll being involved in a murder investigation sometimes took on her.

In the bed Cassandra stirred and sat up, blinking sleepily. "What time is it?" she asked as she reluctantly pushed herself up onto her elbows and pulled the pillows up behind her.

"The sun is up, so I would guess around seven," Jane said, pulling the curtains apart a little to look at the grey sky. "It looks a bit of a dreary morning."

"We cannot have brilliant sunshine every day, I suppose, and it will be a relief not to worry my skin is going pink every time I step outside."

Jane felt Cassandra's eyes on her, studying her with more than a hint of concern.

"What is the plan for today?" Cassandra asked eventually.

Jane shrugged. "It rather depends if Mother and Father allow us to stay, doesn't it?"

"If they had been set on leaving, we would have packed our bags last night. Do not despair, Jane. Sir Phillip might have thought to rile them up with his visit, but he does not know of Father's hatred of being manipulated." She gave Jane a reassuring smile. "Except by you, of course."

"I do not manipulate him," Jane said, aghast at the thought.

"He would never say the words aloud, but you are his favourite, Jane."

"I do not think that is true. He is always saying how lucky he is to have a kind and generous daughter in you, Cassandra."

Cassandra inclined her head but a smile lingered on her lips. "He appreciates all our individual strengths and qualities, but in you he sees a mind to equal his own as well as creativity and passion. Do not think I am jealous, Jane. We are lucky to have such loving and indulgent parents, and I would never begrudge you father's regard. I only bring it up because I think you fret unnecessarily. I am sure he will let us stay and see this thing through to the end."

Jane wasn't convinced. She had seen the fear in her mother's eyes the previous evening. Mr Austen might be the patriarch, but on important matters he would not ignore Mrs Austen's opinion.

"Let us dress and go down for breakfast and stop worrying about things that have not happened as yet."

Downstairs, Mr and Mrs Austen were already seated, talking in low voices with serious expressions. Mr Austen rose as they entered the room.

"Good morning, girls. You have a visitor."

Jane was surprised to see an elderly woman seated next to Mr Austen.

"These are my daughters, Miss Jane Austen and Miss Cassandra Austen," Mr Austen said. "Cassandra, Jane, this is Mrs Agnes Tolbeck. She is the grandmother of the young woman who died a few months ago."

Jane's eyes widened. Mrs Robertson had told her the family had moved away following the young woman's death, but she had evidently not known about the grandmother.

"A pleasure to meet you, Mrs Tolbeck," Jane said, slipping into the seat opposite the elderly woman. Cassandra took a seat next to her.

"I'll get straight to the point," Mrs Tolbeck said in a voice that sounded much younger and stronger than Jane had expected. "My granddaughter, Lily, was found dead five months ago. We had a visit from the magistrate, Mr Margill, and Sir Phillip, the coroner. They sat in my son's kitchen and sympathised with my poor daughter-in-law, but assured us all that Lily's death had been a terrible accident."

Jane considered this. Lily had been the first victim. Back then, there would have been no suspicion of anyone stalking the streets of Lyme Regis and Charmouth, murdering young women. There would have had been no reason to question the verdict of accidental death.

"They were so insistent it was an accident that we had no choice but to believe them. Yet Lily had lived by the sea all her life and was a strong swimmer. It seemed odd to think she could get into trouble so close to the shore, and she certainly knew not to swim near the fishing nets. And yet, when they found her..." Her voice trailed off before she took a deep breath to continue.

"My son and daughter-in-law, Lily's parents, were distraught and when my son got an offer of work in Rye, in Sussex, they moved. I think they just wanted to be able to walk around town without everything reminding them of Lily." Mrs Tolbeck paused. "People are saying there have been three deaths on the beach — including Lily's — and none of them have been accidents." She looked up at Jane with a glimmer of hope in her eyes. "The talk around town is you're going to help find out what really happened."

For a long moment no one in the room spoke, and then Jane reached across the table and took Mrs Tolbeck's hand. The skin was warm and rough, with calluses on her fingers. She was in her sixties, with deep lines on her face and a sadness in her eyes that came with grief. This woman had lost her granddaughter, and then, not long after, her son and daughter-in-law had left the area, unable to stay where the memories of their daughter were too strong.

"As yet I am not sure of anything, but I found the body of Rebecca Robertson on the beach and there were sure signs she had been strangled. Hers was not an accidental death."

"But you are looking into it?"

Jane inclined her head. "I am."

Mrs Tolbeck nodded.

"Can you tell me about Lily?"

Mrs Tolbeck swallowed hard, tears glistening in her eyes. She brushed them away with a determined hand. "Lily was such a beautiful girl. She was seventeen and already she had had a marriage proposal. She loved her ma and pa so much, but she wanted more than the simple life as a fisherman's wife."

Jane studied the woman in front of her and wondered if this was what tied the three victims together. They had all dreamed of a different life, a better life.

"Lily was clever, but not in the conventional sense. She could read a little. I taught her how to form her letters when she was young, although she found it difficult. Her strength was with people. She always knew what to say to make them feel better. Everyone loved her. Her mother would bring her to work on the stall, selling fish, because she was so popular with the customers. She had a way of smiling at you that made you think you were the only person in the whole world."

"Did she have a young man, someone she was walking out with?"

Mrs Tolbeck shook her head. "Not anyone she told us about, but sometimes I wondered. A month before she was killed, young Peter Foster asked her to marry him. He's a handsome lad from a good family. My son hoped she would accept him. Peter is a good fisherman, well respected in Charmouth. It might not have been the life Lily had dreamed of, but I think he would have treated her well and she would have been comfortable."

"She turned him down?"

"She did. Three times, in fact. She told him she was honoured by his interest, but she had different plans for her life. He married Betty Smith a few weeks later." Mrs Tolbeck frowned. "I wasn't too kind to Lily after; I told her she had to accept her lot in life and stop living with her head in the clouds. I said that soon she would get a reputation, and no matter how comely her face and figure the men would stop asking her to marry them. Men don't like to be turned down."

"What did Lily say?"

"She said I needn't worry, that one day she would leave Charmouth and see the world. It wasn't just a dream."

"Did Lily tell you how she might achieve this?"

"No."

Jane closed her eyes for a minute, assimilating the information she had just heard. Lily's story was so similar to that of Eliza Drayson and Rebecca Robertson that it couldn't be a coincidence. All three had likely been involved in a secret relationship, and all three talked of leaving their homes for a better life.

Jane glanced at her parents, who were sitting silently at the table, both looking grave. She knew now was the moment of decision, the moment they would either declare she and Cassandra could stay in Lyme Regis, or that they would leave imminently.

"What do you say?" she asked her father. If he commanded she leave, she would obey his wishes. She had a degree of independence most young women her age could only dream of, but that didn't mean she could completely disregard her parents' opinions.

"A few days," Mr Austen said eventually. "Two, maybe three, and then we must return home. The strain on your mother's nerves will become too much otherwise."

"Thank you," Jane said quietly. She wondered if their decision would have been different if Mrs Tolbeck hadn't arrived at their lodgings that morning with her tale of what had befallen her granddaughter.

"There are a few stipulations," Mr Austen continued. "You do not go anywhere alone, and if your mother or I deem things to be getting too dangerous, you do not argue and we leave immediately."

"Of course," Jane murmured.

"You will find out what happened to my Lily?" Mrs Tolbeck said.

"I will do my very best."

After showing Mrs Tolbeck out, Jane ate only a little of her breakfast, picking at her toast and sipping at her tea as her mind tried to work through the latest information. She was glad when Cassandra declared herself finished and finally they could step out into the cool morning air.

"What did you make of Mrs Tolbeck?" Cassandra asked as they walked arm in arm away from the lodging house.

Jane lowered her voice, aware of the people in the streets, going about their business. Lyme Regis was a small place, and any one of them might be related to the killer. She did not want their discussion unwittingly reported back to the person they hunted.

"I think she was exactly as she seemed," Jane said after a minute. "A grieving grandmother who has suddenly had her whole world ripped from her."

"I am surprised she did not move with her son and daughter-in-law."

"I expect there was some practical reason why she could not. Perhaps she continues to run the fish stall, or maybe she simply did not want to leave her home."

"Poor woman," Cassandra said, shaking her head.

"Her information did throw up some interesting points, though, in particular the timeline of events. In my mind I have been thinking of Lily as victim number one, Eliza as victim number two and Rebecca as victim number three. Yet if we believe the killer to be the father of Eliza's second child, then he must have started a relationship with her first. He then later became involved with Lily. He killed Lily before killing Eliza a few months later. We do not know when he became involved with Rebecca, since Francesca only became aware of the relationship in the last few weeks."

Cassandra shivered. "The killer must be very charming. The three women might have been poor, but they were all pretty and desirable. Lily had received a marriage proposal, and from the sound of it Rebecca was expected to marry well too."

Jane thought about what sort of man the murderer could be. Most of her acquaintances were women, and the only men she knew well were her brothers. They were very different in their personalities and their habits, but all had good hearts. "Either he is very good at covering what he is doing, or someone close to him knows there is something going on. If he has any family or friends then they must suspect something."

He would have a mother, a brother or a sister perhaps, someone who loved and cherished him, someone who would not want to believe the terrible things he was capable of but perhaps harboured a seed of suspicion somewhere deep inside them.

"Perhaps he keeps himself to himself," Cassandra said, and Jane let out a frustrated groan.

"This should be straightforward. Three victims — find the person that connects them and we should have our murderer."

CHAPTER ELEVEN

Jane was becoming familiar with the walk over the cliffs to Charmouth and today, with the weather cooler the sun hiding behind the clouds, she enjoyed the pleasant stroll with Cassandra. Captain Robertson accompanied them, but had been quiet for much of the walk, lost in his thoughts.

"How does your mother fare?" Jane asked as they began the descent to Charmouth.

"She could not get out of bed this morning. Francesca took her some breakfast, but half an hour later the tray was untouched."

"And you?" Jane enquired.

"I would rest easier if we could identify my sister's killer. As it is, I cannot sleep. I feel a great fury that this man is out there, walking the streets whilst Rebecca lies cold, ready for the grave."

"Anger is to be expected," Jane said, glancing up at the young man's face. His brows were furrowed and he looked pale and drawn; the emotional toll was clearly visible. "Will you be granted any additional leave from the army?"

"No. I have a couple more weeks and then it will be back to my regiment."

Jane wondered if she detected a hint of relief in his voice. She couldn't blame him. At least with his regiment he would be kept busy, with no time to dwell on his sister's fate or to see his mother wasting away as she fell into a deep melancholy.

They walked through the pretty streets of Charmouth to a neat row of houses close to the harbour. Captain Robertson paused outside them, studying the façades while he tried to recall which one they wanted.

After a moment he selected a door and knocked on it, waiting only briefly before it was opened. A young woman stood inside, her hair pulled back into a loose bun and an apron over her simple brown dress. She looked up at Captain Robertson and then promptly burst into tears.

"Miss Ringwood," Captain Robertson said, "please accept my apologies for calling unannounced."

"It is true then?"

"It is true."

There were fresh tears on the young woman's cheeks as she ushered them inside.

Captain Robertson made the introductions. "This is Miss Jane Austen and her sister, Miss Cassandra Austen. They are helping me look into Rebecca's death."

"My father told me yesterday of the news. I spent half the night awake and praying he had got it wrong, that it wasn't Rebecca." She took a deep, shuddering breath before continuing. "I can't believe it. I only saw her a few days ago."

She led them through to a small sitting room with a sofa and two armchairs, indicating they should sit.

"I will make some tea."

"We hoped to talk to you about Rebecca," Jane said quickly. "I gather you and Miss Hettie Wright were her friends."

"Hettie only lives three doors down. Shall I fetch her?"

"That would be helpful."

Lucy Ringwood disappeared and they heard the front door opening and closing. For a few minutes they sat in silence before the door opened again and another young woman accompanied Lucy into the house.

"Captain Robertson," Hettie said as she entered the room. "I am so sorry for your loss. I was devastated when I heard the news."

Hettie was another pretty young woman and Jane suspected the three friends — Rebecca, Hettie and Lucy — had been the envy of many of the other girls at Miss Warkworth's School for Young Ladies. Lucy had fair hair and delicate features whereas Hettie was taller, with dark eyes and dark hair.

Captain Robertson made the introductions again and Lucy returned a few minutes later with a teapot and cups, busying herself with pouring the tea.

"Rebecca had been seeing someone secretly," Captain Robertson said when they were settled, steaming cups of tea in everyone's hands. "We found sketches someone had drawn of her, and Francesca caught her sneaking out to meet someone."

"We hoped you might know who it was," Jane added.

Lucy and Hettie exchanged glances before Hettie shook her head. Jane felt a wave of irritation, wondering if they were trying to protect the memory of their friend, or someone else.

"I know it may feel like you are betraying her confidence, to speak out about what you know, but Rebecca was in all likelihood killed by this man she thought loved her."

"She didn't tell us who it was," Hettie said, biting her lip. "It was all very mysterious, but I got the impression the secrecy added to the excitement of the courtship."

"When did it start, do you know?"

Hettie leaned forwards, placing her cup of tea on the little table to one side of her chair. "She wouldn't tell us anything, but if I had to guess I would say a few months ago. We would arrange to meet Rebecca on the cliffs or the beach in Lyme Regis, or she would walk over to visit us here. A little over three months ago she missed a few visits. I didn't think anything of it at first, but when we saw her next she was distracted. She was excited about something."

"Did you question her about it?"

"Yes, and eventually she admitted she had met someone, but she would not give us any more information than that."

"We pressed her time and again. Normally we shared everything." Lucy shook her head. "Not this time."

Lucy tugged at the sleeves of her dress.

"When did you last see Rebecca?"

"Last week," Lucy answered. "She came to visit, and Hettie popped in for tea."

"How did she seem?"

Lucy and Hettie exchanged glances.

"Happy," Hettie said eventually. "She couldn't stop smiling, and when I asked her what had occurred she said she would soon be able to tell us everything."

Jane felt a knot twist in her stomach and wondered if this development had prompted Rebecca's death. If Rebecca had pressed her gentleman to allow her to reveal his identity it could have been the reason he had killed her, silencing her before anyone found out who he was.

"She said we would not believe what she was going to tell us."

"I think that is significant," Jane said. "It suggests she was going to tell you she was involved with someone of a certain status or reputation that you would find astonishing, or perhaps he was someone you already knew but would not imagine her to be with."

At Jane's words Hettie cleared her throat. "We did speculate, of course, between ourselves. We spoke of every man we knew between the ages of sixteen and sixty, but there was one name we kept coming back to."

Jane held her breath. This could be the moment they heard the name of the murderer.

Lucy gripped Hettie's arm, looking uncomfortable. "That isn't to say we think he is the man who killed Rebecca. I don't want to throw baseless accusations about. It isn't fair to him."

Next to her Jane felt Captain Robertson shift and could sense he was beginning to lose patience with the two young women. They must have sensed it too, for Hettie spoke. "Miss Warkworth saw to most of our instruction at school. She taught us deportment and the basics of housekeeping and music. There was a young lady who came once a week to teach us needlework, Miss Springer." She paused. "Then there was Monsieur Etienne. Jacques."

"Jacques?"

"We used to call him Monsieur Etienne when Miss Warkworth was around, but once the classroom door closed he said we could call him Jacques."

"That's very familiar."

Lucy shook her head vehemently. "It's continental. Jacques told us that in France all tutors are addressed by their given names. It fosters an equality between the student and the teacher and allows for more intimate and useful discussion."

Jane had attended school a few years earlier, an establishment for young ladies not dissimilar to the one Rebecca and her friends had attended. There had been some time spent on literature and music, but much of what they had learned had been how to run a household and make themselves desirable as a potential spouse. She had hated Tuesday afternoons spent perfecting their needlework and had often wished she could attend the same schools as her brothers, where academia was the focus instead of domestic pursuits.

"Jacques taught you French?"

"He did, French and art. He was an artist, a very talented one, but he'd left Paris because of the unrest and escaped to England to live in peace and pursue his art."

"It sounds like you know a lot about him."

Lucy gave a defiant shrug. "He treated us like adults, like equals. Miss Warkworth spent the whole time we were at school barking instructions at us and finding something to criticise. Jacques was different."

"Did he pay any special attention to Rebecca?"

Hettie glanced at Lucy before answering. "He liked Rebecca…" she began slowly, choosing her words carefully. "He used to spend a long time talking to her about watercolours and sketching, and sometimes they would go for strolls together around the garden during our art lessons."

"How old is he?" Captain Robertson asked, a hard edge to his voice.

Lucy shrugged. "Not old. Perhaps twenty-seven or twenty-eight."

"There wasn't anything improper," Hettie added quickly.

"Just a teacher going for private walks with one of his pupils," Cassandra murmured.

Lucy turned to her sharply and shook her head. "You're wrong, Miss Austen. Jacques had no interest in Rebecca like that. He admired her artistic ability and enjoyed talking to her, but there was no romantic interest."

"Was there someone he was romantically involved with?"

Lucy shrugged. "I don't think so."

"Does he lived at the school?"

"Yes, he has a cottage there."

"Do *you* think he could have been Rebecca's admirer?" Jane addressed the question to Hettie. Lucy clearly held the French teacher in high regard, but Hettie seemed more sensible.

"He was fond of Rebecca. She was very beautiful, of course, and she had something about her, this spark that drew people in. Sometimes I thought I saw him watching her when we were in class."

"Hettie!" Lucy exclaimed, shaking her head. "That's not true."

"Not often, only once or twice. Of course we left Miss Warkworth's last year, so Rebecca was no longer his pupil."

"Did you ever see them together after that?"

"Once, on the beach. Lucy and I were out for a stroll and there they were, walking together. Rebecca later brushed it off and said they had bumped into one another, nothing more, and she was merely being polite." Hettie shrugged. "So perhaps there is nothing in it."

Lucy glared around the room. "You can't hound him. He has already been through so much. It wouldn't be right and it wouldn't be fair." She folded her arms across her body, a fierce expression on her face.

"No one is going to hound anyone," Jane said soothingly. "But I expect if Monsieur Etienne held Rebecca in such high regard, he will be only too pleased to tell us what he knows."

"Is there anyone else?" Cassandra enquired. "You said you considered every man you knew; are there any other possibilities, however unlikely they seem?"

"There was Billy Asker. He always doffed his cap and would blush whenever Rebecca passed him in the street," Lucy said quickly.

"Billy Asker is barely twenty. I don't think Rebecca would ever have looked twice at him," said Hettie.

"And there's Mr Gough — he's a widower and Rebecca once said he was the most handsome man in Charmouth."

Hettie again did not look convinced, shaking her head.

"Or Lord Willingham," Lucy continued.

"Now you're being ridiculous."

"Lord Willingham?" Jane said, her interest piqued.

"He's almost old enough to be her grandfather," Hettie said and gave a meaningful look to Lucy, inclining her head to where Captain Robertson sat.

"I am sorry, Captain Robertson," Lucy said, dampening her enthusiasm for her latest suspect. "I did not mean to be disrespectful. It's just that even Rebecca used to find it strange how generous he was. Paying for your commission and Rebecca and Francesca's schooling. Discounts on the rent and gifts each Christmas."

"He is a generous man," Captain Robertson said.

"Did Rebecca ever indicate there was anything more to it than that?" Jane said.

"No," Hettie replied quickly. "She said Lord Willingham was interested in her schooling and if she encountered him in the street, he would enquire about her health and education, but nothing more."

Jane nodded, filing the information away. Relationships with great age differences were not unusual, but she could not see Rebecca dreaming of running away and starting a fresh and exciting new chapter of her life with a man approaching sixty.

"There was young Mr Willingham as well," Lucy said, seeming determined to mention any man Rebecca had encountered in a bid to protect Jacques Etienne.

"Thomas?" Captain Robertson said.

"Yes. I saw them talking once on the cliffs when I was walking over to meet her in Lyme Regis. When he had left, she said he was back from university and was enquiring as to the health of her family."

Hettie rolled her eyes and stood up, collecting the empty cups. "Hardly the talk between two besotted lovers," she muttered as she cleared everything away to the kitchen at the back of the house.

"You know Thomas Willingham?" Jane asked Captain Robertson.

"Yes, I used to play with the Willingham boys when I was young. Rupert, the eldest, more than Thomas, but Thomas sometimes too." The captain shrugged. "I cannot see his path crossing with Rebecca's much, let alone Eliza or Lily."

Jane turned back to the two young women. "Did either of you know Eliza Drayson or Lily Tolbeck?"

"I knew Lily," Hettie said. "Her father is a fisherman, and I don't think she got much in the way of schooling, but I would play with her on the beach sometimes when we were children. I did not know Eliza Drayson."

Lucy wrinkled her nose. "Rebecca did," she said. "She said hello to her if we were out and about, even when everyone else crossed the street."

"Is there anything else you think might help?" Jane asked.

The two young women sat and contemplated for a moment before both shaking their heads.

"The funeral is tomorrow at ten o'clock. I know my mother would appreciate it if you came. Rebecca spoke of you both so fondly," Captain Robertson said as Lucy showed them out. Jane could see the strain on his face. It must be particularly hard seeing Rebecca's friends, so young and full of life, knowing Rebecca would never sit and laugh and drink tea with them ever again.

CHAPTER TWELVE

"Please wait," Jane called, running to catch up with Captain Robertson. He was moving fast, his long legs striding down the street as if a wild dog nipped at his heels.

"It may be better if you do not accompany me, Miss Austen."

"Nonsense."

"You do not want to be party to what happens next."

"Take a moment," Jane pleaded. "Think this through. All we have is the suspicion of one young woman. Monsieur Etienne may be entirely innocent. He may merely be an enthusiastic teacher who takes an interest in the students he teaches."

Captain Robertson scoffed and continued at his relentless pace. Jane could hear Cassandra hurrying behind them, barely able to keep up.

"Please, Captain," Cassandra called. "We need to do this the right way."

Cassandra's quiet but insistent voice breached his defences for a moment and he paused, turning to face the two sisters.

"If we barrel in and scare him, he will not tell us anything. As yet there is no evidence he is the man we seek, just the speculation of a young woman who may be wrong. We need to approach this carefully, step lightly without throwing accusations. That way we can assess him, get the measure of the man."

"He might have killed Rebecca," Captain Robertson said, trailing a hand through his normally neat hair. Now it was sticking up, whipped by the wind and his agitated movements.

"Hitting him may well make you feel better for a few seconds, but that feeling will not last when he refuses to tell us anything or, worse, flees the area and cannot be found."

"What do you suggest, Miss Austen?"

"Let Cassandra and I speak to him alone first. He works with young women and from how Lucy and Hettie spoke of him, I think he must have a certain charm. His guard will be lower with us; he will think he can influence our thinking." She saw the displeasure on the captain's face and continued quickly. "All I ask for is ten minutes."

Captain Robertson didn't answer for a long moment and then gave a short, sharp nod. "Fine. Ten minutes, no more. I will wait outside."

"Thank you." Jane breathed a sigh of relief.

"The school is on the outskirts of the town." He set off at a brisk pace again and Jane was glad for the cooler temperatures. Walking so fast in heat like that of the previous few days would have meant she arrived at the school perspiring.

Miss Warkworth's School for Young Ladies was a smart building of grey stone with an imposing façade. It was larger than Jane had expected, although with several girls boarding at the school and an equal number of day pupils it needed to be big enough to accommodate them all. She had imagined something small and quaint, a country school for the wealthier of the local girls, but it looked more like an institution you would find in one of the larger towns.

Their knock on the door was answered by an elderly man who shuffled away once Jane had introduced herself and Cassandra, mumbling an instruction to wait where they were. Jane had asked to speak to Miss Warkworth first, before Monsieur Etienne.

A few minutes later a woman in her forties appeared. She looked every inch a headmistress with her grey-streaked hair pulled back into a tight bun and her high-necked, dark grey dress. She was frowning as she approached, but invited them into a neat little parlour without asking any further questions.

"Thank you for seeing us," Jane said as she settled into her seat. Miss Warkworth did not offer them any refreshment, and Jane suspected the schoolmistress would only give them a limited amount of time. After introductions she launched straight into an explanation of why they were there. "Miss Robertson's family have asked my sister and I to gather any information we can that might help the authorities in establishing events leading up to her death."

"How unusual," Miss Warkworth murmured, but motioned for Jane to continue.

"I know Miss Robertson left your school last year, but I think you must know the young ladies in your care very well and hoped you might have a unique understanding of Miss Robertson."

Miss Warkworth sighed and looked down at her hands for a moment, but when she raised her eyes to meet Jane's there was a steely determination in them.

"This is a horrific matter," she said, her words clipped but firm. "The death of anyone is a tragedy, but Miss Robertson was one of life's true shining lights. She was a beautiful young woman, but there was much more to her than that. She was compassionate and had an enquiring mind. We expected much from her."

"What did she plan to do with her future?"

"Marry, of course," Miss Warkworth said, with a raised eyebrow. "There are some of us in this world that have a different calling, but we should not sneer at the young ladies who follow a more traditional path."

"Miss Robertson left school last year, I understand."

"Yes. I had expected her to be married by now, but sometimes the *right* offer takes a little time to materialise."

"Had you seen her in the past year?"

"Of course. We are a small community here in Charmouth and Lyme Regis. I saw her at plenty of events over the last year. My former pupils always spare a moment to talk and tell me about their progress out in the world."

"When did you last see Miss Robertson?"

Miss Warkworth thought for a moment. "Three weeks ago. It was glorious weather, and I went for a walk on the cliffs after church. Miss Robertson was out walking with Miss Lucy Ringwood. They were always close friends at school and they were walking arm in arm along the cliffs."

"Just the two of them?"

"Yes," said Miss Warkworth, smiling shrewdly. "Miss Hettie Wright normally makes up their little group, but she was absent."

"How did Miss Robertson seem?"

"She was happy, eager to talk about her brother returning home on leave in a few weeks and her sister Francesca, who is a pupil at the school." Miss Warkworth tilted her head to one side. "I spoke more to Miss Ringwood, if I am honest. Miss Ringwood lost her mother about six months ago and has fallen into the role of housekeeper for her father. I offered her some words of wisdom about not getting stuck in an unhappy situation."

"Were you aware of anyone courting Miss Robertson?"

"No. It was a point of concern from her mother. She has been most eager for Miss Robertson to make a good match, to marry up the social ladder as it were. The late Mr Robertson worked for Lord Willingham, as a groundskeeper or in some such position. Their good fortune in recent years has been thanks to the generosity of the baron rather than the social class they were born into." There was a hint of superiority to Miss Warkworth's words, and Jane wondered if the headmistress had not particularly liked Miss Robertson. She would not speak ill of her, but there was a hint of disapproval.

"Mrs Robertson hoped for a better match for her daughter?"

"Yes. Most of the parents of the girls I teach do. It is the reason they send them to my school, to gain those little accomplishments that set them apart from the other young women vying for a bachelor's attention. None of my girls are very wealthy, but their parents have enough money to understand that an investment in their daughters' educations will be a wise decision in the long run."

"Yet Miss Ringwood, Miss Wright and Miss Robertson all remain unmarried," Jane said, unable to help herself.

"There is no point rushing into an unwise decision. I advocate for weighing up one's options and making a sensible decision. I am sure in time Miss Wright and Miss Ringwood will marry."

"Can you think of anyone who might want to hurt Miss Robertson?" Jane asked. "Any enemies or people she had quarrelled with?"

Miss Warkworth let out a short, mirthless laugh. "You do have some strange ideas, Miss Austen. Miss Robertson had no enemies. She was a seventeen-year-old girl who had never left Dorset. Of course she quarrelled — put a dozen young ladies together in an establishment and force them to spend time together and there will always be arguments, but these were the petty kind."

"What sort of arguments?"

Miss Warkworth gave a long-suffering sigh before continuing. "A few years ago, Miss Robertson accused Miss Polly Upton of stealing some ribbons she used to like wearing in her hair. The ribbons were found, but the friendship between the two girls never recovered. Then there were the tiffs between Miss Robertson and her closest friends, over trivial matters no doubt."

"With Miss Ringwood and Miss Wright?"

"Yes, but as I say over very trivial matters, and as the girls matured these quarrels all but disappeared."

Jane thought back to her time at school. She had insisted her father send her when Cassandra had gone, a little earlier than her mother would have liked. It had been a wonderful experience, but she had been lucky to have gone through it all with Cassandra. Together they had navigated the unspoken rules and expectations, worked out who to associate with and who to avoid. It had made the period enjoyable rather than painful.

"Thank you for your time, Miss Warkworth. I wonder if we might speak to your other teachers now."

"The school is only a small establishment. I provide most of the instruction. We also have Monsieur Etienne on site, who teaches the girls French and Art."

"Can we speak to him?"

"Of course. I will take you to his set of rooms. They are in the grounds but separate from the school building itself. It would not be proper for a male teacher to be in the same building as the girls, although I myself have my room on the same floor as their dormitory to ensure there is no sneaking about at night."

"Thank you."

They followed Miss Warkworth out of the parlour and through the school building, leaving through the back door that led out into an extensive garden. Close to the house was a kitchen garden where no doubt the young ladies learned to plant and tend to small crops of herbs, fruit and vegetables. Like everything else in the school, it looked neat and well looked after.

"Monsieur Etienne has been here for three years. He is wonderful with the girls and allows us to broaden our curriculum to include French and Art."

"Did he know Miss Robertson particularly well?"

"No more so than any other pupil here. He is a professional, Miss Austen, and does not have favourites."

Jane doubted this was true. Every teacher had a student they favoured above the others, often one that was talented and amiable, but sometimes it was a mere matter of a personality. They also had pupils they disliked, the ones who made their lives harder in the classroom.

Miss Warkworth knocked on the door of a small cottage that stood to one side. It looked as though it had first been built for a gardener and even now had beautiful roses trained up a wooden frame next to the door.

The door opened and a man appeared. He was dressed casually, with his sleeves rolled up and the neck of his shirt open, revealing tanned skin.

"Monsieur Etienne," Miss Warkworth said. "This is Miss Jane Austen and Miss Cassandra Austen. They are asking some questions about poor Miss Robertson on behalf of her family."

Monsieur Etienne stepped out into the light, and Jane felt her eyes widen a little. It was impossible to deny the teacher was a very attractive man. Somewhere in his late twenties, he had a muscular build and a handsome face that was transformed into something even more striking when he smiled.

"It is a pleasure to meet you," he said, turning the full force of his charm on Jane and Cassandra. His expression turned serious again. "It is a terrible tragedy and I will do anything I can to help." He glanced back over his shoulder to the dark interior of his cottage and then motioned towards the garden. "There is a lovely spot in the orchard. I think we will be more comfortable there."

"Thank you for your help, Miss Warkworth," Jane said, keen the headmistress did not accompany them whilst they questioned Monsieur Etienne.

Miss Warkworth watched them as they wove through the kitchen garden and then onto the grass beyond. The grounds of the small school were not extensive, and after a moderate-sized lawn there was a gate to a small orchard. Around twenty apple trees stood in rows, heavy with fruit, and there were a few benches sitting in the shade of the trees.

"Will you be comfortable here?" Monsieur Etienne asked, motioning towards a well-positioned bench. It sat at the edge of the orchard, looking out over the rolling countryside beyond the school grounds. There was a felled tree trunk lying a few feet away, opposite the bench, and Monsieur Etienne sat there rather than crowding onto the bench with Cassandra and Jane.

"I was devastated to hear about the death of Miss Robertson. The world is a poorer place without her in it."

"You knew her well?"

"Yes, of course. I taught her French and Art, two very intimate subjects. Miss Robertson was a particularly talented artist."

Jane thought of the sketches hidden away in Rebecca Roberson's cushion cover and felt her heart begin to pound in her chest. Monsieur Etienne seemed genuinely devastated about Rebecca's death, but it did not mean he wasn't involved.

"When did you last see her?"

He contemplated the question for a moment and then nodded quickly. "I do remember. Two weeks ago. She walked over the cliffs to meet her sister and accompany her home. I was heading to the beach, so I walked with Miss Robertson for a few minutes whilst her younger sister went ahead with friends. We saw Miss Ringwood as well, in the distance, but she was heading away from us."

"You haven't seen her since?"

"No." He spread his hands. "I am much occupied by my work here at the school, and I spend the rest of my time on my art."

"What do you do, Monsieur Etienne?" Cassandra asked, her expression one of genuine interest. Momentarily Jane marvelled at how well her sister had learned to dissemble and deceive in the last couple of years. "Paint? Draw?"

"A little of both. I sketch, but my main passion is oil painting. Unfortunately, the paints are expensive and not readily available in a place such as this."

"I understand you came here from Paris," Jane said, trying to make her tone light.

"Yes, although originally I am from a little village in the south of France. One day I would like to return to Paris, but not yet. People have long memories. For now I am content I have a job I enjoy and just enough funds to pursue my passions."

Jane leaned forward and lowered her voice, as if taking Monsieur Etienne into her confidence. "It must be challenging, working in a school full of young women. I am sure one or two have developed an affection for you."

Monsieur Etienne shrugged. "Of course, I think it is only to be expected."

"How do you deal with that, may I ask?"

"I ignore it. I have found most of these infatuations are short-lived if you do nothing to stoke the flames. The girls grow up and move on."

"Was there anything of the sort with Rebecca Robertson?"

He looked up sharply. "No, Miss Austen. I admit I liked Miss Robertson — as a pupil, you understand. She was intelligent and had true artistic talent. Sometimes we would take a stroll together and discuss art, talk about the great masters, their paintings, but there was nothing more than that." He held out his hands, his expression sincere. "I value my job too much to ever think of any of the young ladies as anything more than pupils."

He was convincing, so much so that Jane felt a stab of disappointment. With the suspicions of Hettie Wright and the sketches they had found in Rebecca's room, she had thought they might have found their killer, but instead he seemed a reasonable man who was well aware of the perils of living and working in an environment where he was the only man.

"Please excuse the personal nature of these questions," Jane said, giving her most reassuring smile. "You are not obliged to tell me anything, of course, but as I am sure you understand there are rumours swirling and I simply seek to reassure Miss Robertson's family."

Monsieur Etienne assumed a relaxed posture and nodded amicably. "I have nothing to hide, Miss Austen. Please, ask your questions."

"Are you currently courting someone?"

He tried to suppress a smile. "I am an artist, Miss Austen. It is not in my nature to court a young woman."

"An affair then?" Jane said, refusing to be embarrassed and desperately hoping she would not blush.

"I have had a few affairs whilst I have been here in Charmouth, but nothing lasting."

"Are you engaged in an affair currently?"

"No, Miss Austen. You will find no one in my bed in the early hours of the morning at the moment."

"Did you know a young woman by the name of Eliza Drayson?"

"I have heard of her. She was found dead a few weeks ago, I believe."

"But you did not know her?"

"No."

"How about a young woman called Lily Tolbeck?"

"Ah," he said, shifting his position slightly. It was the first time he had looked uncomfortable. "Lily I did know."

"Lily wasn't a pupil here, so may I ask how you knew her?"

"She sat for me a few times, as a model."

Jane raised an eyebrow. It hadn't been the answer she was expecting. "A model?"

"She was very beautiful and I fancied she would make a good Juliet."

"Juliet?"

"I wanted to paint the balcony scene from Shakespeare's *Romeo and Juliet*." He shrugged. "She posed for me half a dozen times, but in the end I could not get the proportions right. I paid her for her time but didn't ask her to come back."

"When was this?"

He thought for a minute before answering. "About six months ago."

"A month before she died?"

"Yes. I was shaken by her death. She was such a warm and beautiful young lady."

Jane studied Monsieur Etienne. His demeanour was relaxed and his answers seemed truthful, but Jane had to remind herself that the man they were seeking had deceived three women, gained their trust and made them fall in love with him before brutally murdering them. Such a man would have to be a good liar.

"There is one more thing," Jane said slowly. "A small cache of drawings were found in Miss Robertson's room after her death, secreted away so no one would come across them whilst she was alive. They are drawings of her, and they look like they were drawn by someone who cared for her. Did you ever draw Miss Robertson?"

"No," he said quickly. "Never. As I said earlier, I am no fool. I am aware of the infatuations the girls here develop, and I try to do nothing that would encourage one to think they are higher in my favour than any other."

Jane recalled Hettie saying Monsieur Etienne had paid Rebecca particular attention, how they had taken walks together and discussed art. Perhaps he didn't realise this was a form of favouritism, or perhaps, despite his assurances to the contrary, he liked being surrounded by pretty young women who hung on his every word.

"Thank you for your help, Monsieur Etienne," Jane said as she and Cassandra stood. They smoothed down their skirts and Monsieur Etienne stood, bowed and then led them back through the gardens. He showed them through a side gate so they could pass directly out onto the road beyond, without having to go through the school building.

"I do hope you find the man you are looking for," he said as he raised a hand to bid them farewell.

CHAPTER THIRTEEN

They found Captain Robertson sitting on a wall near the sea, looking broodily out at the water.

"What did you find out?" he asked. Jane was pleased to see he had lost some of the fury that had been driving him before she and Cassandra had persuaded him they were better talking to the French teacher alone.

"Monsieur Etienne denied knowing your sister in any capacity except as her teacher," Jane said. "He knew Lily Tolbeck, but said he had never met Eliza Drayson."

"He could have been lying."

"Of course he could." Jane paused. "He also denied ever drawing your sister, so we cannot assume the pictures were his."

"He is an artist, the only artist we know," Captain Robertson said, his voice hard. "Of course he denies the drawings are his."

He went to stand and Jane had visions of him storming into Miss Warkworth's School for Young Ladies and demanding satisfaction at dawn. She placed a calming hand on his arm.

"Wait," she said, her fingers pressing against the stiff material of his jacket. "There are things we can do to confirm or refute his story. The man is not going anywhere. Let us pick away at the things he said, pull at the threads and see if anything comes loose."

For a dreadful moment she thought he might refuse, then he nodded and sank back against the wall.

"Whilst we are here, I thought we might call on Peter Foster," Jane said.

"The young man who asked Lily Tolbeck to marry him?" Cassandra said.

"Yes. Lily's grandmother told us he is a fisherman here in Charmouth. He is married to someone else now, but he must have spent some time with Lily in the months before she died. Perhaps she let slip something about the man she was hoping to spend her life with instead of him."

Captain Robertson nodded. "If he is a fisherman, then he will keep his boat in the harbour here. He might still be out on his boat, though. The fishermen often go out in the early hours of the morning, but depending on how good their catch is they might stay out until mid-morning or late afternoon."

"It is worth looking," Jane said, pleased to have diverted Captain Robertson for a short time.

They walked towards the harbour and within a few minutes the little bobbing boats could be seen beyond the protective harbour wall. Captain Robertson volunteered to go and enquire as to where they might find Peter Foster, and Jane and Cassandra stood looking out to sea.

"What did you make of Monsieur Etienne?" Jane asked her sister now they were alone.

"He was very charming, wasn't he? He tried hard not to be, I think, for our sake."

"I got that impression too. I imagine his usual manner is to flatter and tease young ladies, but because of the nature of our conversation he tried to appear sincere and respectable."

"I cannot believe he doesn't enjoy the attention he gets from being surrounded by a dozen infatuated young ladies," Cassandra said. "None of that means he killed Rebecca, Lily and Eliza, though, does it?"

Jane shook her head. There were some tenuous connections — the favour he displayed towards Rebecca in her final months at the school, and the drawings found in her room that had been done by a talented artist — but there was nothing definite. He denied even knowing Eliza Drayson, and Jane was inclined to believe him. Eliza lived in Lyme Regis and he in Charmouth, and there was no convincing evidence that their paths had ever even crossed.

"I do not think we can definitively say he is the murderer," Jane said, dropping her voice as Captain Robertson approached. "Yet I am not happy to strike him from the list of potential suspects as yet."

They fell silent as Captain Robertson came within earshot. He paused in front of them and nodded at a little boat just making its way into the harbour.

"We're in luck: that's Peter Foster's boat. He should be moored within a few minutes, and we can question him then."

Before they could reach the boat, a young woman had come bustling along the harbour wall and jumped aboard, talking to the man behind the wheel. Their conversation was lively but came to a halt as Jane, Cassandra and Captain Robertson approached.

"Good morning," Jane said, wondering what the etiquette was for stepping onto someone's boat and whether you had to wait to be asked. "My name is Miss Jane Austen, and this is my sister Miss Cassandra Austen." She motioned behind her to where Captain Robertson stood. "You may know Captain Robertson."

"Our condolences," the man said, nodding grimly at the captain. "We heard of what happened to your sister. The whole town is in shock."

"Thank you."

Mr Foster stood looking up at them warily and Jane pushed on quickly. "I hoped we might take a few minutes of your time to ask you some questions about Lily Tolbeck."

Mr Foster blew out his cheeks and cast a glance at the woman beside him.

"Don't give me that look," she said, shaking her head in an all-knowing fashion. "I told you Lily Tolbeck was more trouble than she was worth."

"This is my wife, Betty," Mr Foster said in introduction. "We've been wed a few months now."

"After Lily Tolbeck turned him down and broke his heart," said Mrs Foster.

"Don't be soft in the head," Mr Foster said, and Jane thought she detected a hint of a blush on his cheeks. "Lily didn't break my heart."

"I understand you proposed to Lily," Jane said.

"Three times," Mrs Foster said with a shake of her head. "You'd think this fool would have stopped after being turned down twice."

"Hush, woman."

"Why do you want to know about Lily Tolbeck?" Mrs Foster asked, hands on her hips now. Her stance wasn't combative, yet Jane got the impression she was ready to defend her husband if the situation called for it.

Jane cleared her throat, taking a moment to decide how much to tell this couple. She had to assume anything she said would be spread around Charmouth and Lyme Regis by dinnertime.

"The authorities are investigating Miss Tolbeck's death alongside Miss Robertson's. The coroner and magistrate think there might be a link between them."

"Lily drowned."

"Her grandmother told us she was an excellent swimmer."

Mr Foster looked uncomfortable. "She was. She used to swim in the sea when she was a girl, but that doesn't mean she didn't drown. The sea has strong currents around here; even the strongest of swimmers can be caught unawares and swept out. When that happens, you panic, and then there is no hope whatsoever."

"Look at their faces, Peter," Mrs Foster said quietly. "Lily didn't drown."

Mr Foster gripped the boat's wheel tighter before giving a resolute nod. "Ask me whatever you want."

"You knew Lily well?" Jane began as Mr Foster and his wife stepped off the boat and joined them on dry land.

"I did. Her father was a fisherman, just like mine. We're a small community here in Charmouth and we stick together. If one fisherman has a problem with his nets, everyone groups together to mend them. No fisherman or his family will ever go hungry when another boat has brought in a good catch."

"You knew her family?"

"Yes. She was a few years younger than me, but she would sometimes accompany her dad on the boat, just like I would go out with mine on our boat."

"Did you court her?"

"No," Mr Foster said with a frown. "Although not for want of trying. I asked her to walk out with me on a Sunday after church a few times, but she always found an excuse. In the end I decided I would just ask her to marry me."

"She turned you down?"

"Yes. That time and twice more. She was kind about it, but she told me she wanted more from life than what I could offer her."

"It is hard work — early mornings and physical labour," Mrs Foster said, looking grimly at the boat.

Mr Foster reached out and took her hand. "I know how lucky I am to have you by my side, Betty."

"Lily Tolbeck was a dreamer," Mrs Foster said, shaking her head sadly.

"We think she may have secretly been courting someone. Do you have any idea who this may have been?"

Mr Foster sighed and looked off into the distance. He was not one to hide his thoughts, with every emotion visible on his face. "I suspected there might have been someone. She was always coy about it and never said anything outright, but the last time I asked her to marry me she said she wasn't planning on being in Charmouth for long."

"There's more. Tell them, Peter," Mrs Foster urged.

"There was one evening, a few weeks before she died, when I saw her walking through the town. I didn't follow her exactly, but it was cold and getting dark and she seemed to be acting strangely. I wanted to be sure she wasn't in danger."

Jane nodded, feeling a frisson of excitement spark inside her. It felt like this could be a key moment.

"She walked up the hill, looked around to make sure she wasn't observed, and then slipped into the grounds of Miss Warkworth's school."

For a moment no one said anything, and then Captain Robertson let out a low growl. Jane laid a hand on his arm, trying to calm him.

"We do not know it was a romantic liaison," she said quickly. "Monsieur Etienne told us Lily sat for him as a model a few times. He was painting her."

Captain Robertson snorted and shook Jane's hand off. "If you believe that, Miss Austen, then you are too naïve in the ways of the world." He turned back to Mr Foster. "Did you see who she met?"

"No, the garden was in darkness, and once I had seen her slip inside there was nothing more I could do."

"Thank you for telling us, Mr Foster."

"Lily Tolbeck was a sweet girl," he said, the sadness visible on his face. "She had her whole life ahead of her. If someone did do this to her, if someone killed her, I hope you find him and he hangs for his crimes."

Mr and Mrs Foster climbed back onto the little boat and began sorting the nets that were laid on the deck.

"I am going to see this scoundrel and confront him," Captain Robertson said, his expression determined.

"We have no evidence. He admitted he knew Lily as well as your sister — he didn't hide that from us."

"You believe he painted her, nothing more? Surely you are not as innocent as all that, Miss Austen. You must have heard of the reputation of artists. They spend their lives seducing women, using their art as a reason to get them alone and then promising them the hedonistic life of an artist's muse." His voice caught in his throat. "If he debased Rebecca like that…"

"We need to move cautiously. The last thing we want to do is alert him to our suspicions," Jane said. She wasn't ruling Monsieur Etienne out as a suspect, but when they had interviewed him she hadn't been convinced of his guilt either.

"No, no more caution. I will go to the school myself and ask the cad what he did to Rebecca."

Before Jane could stop him Captain Robertson strode off, moving so fast he was off the harbour wall in no time at all.

"What do we do?" Cassandra asked, looking alarmed.

"I do not think we can stop him, but we should follow him and be there to pick up the pieces when he gets thrown out of the school."

They hurried after him, losing sight of him after a minute as he wound his way through the streets back towards Miss Warkworth's School for Young Ladies.

When they arrived at the building, the front door was open and inside a gaggle of young girls stood chattering excitedly. Jane exchanged a glance with Cassandra and then as one they hurried into the school and out the door at the back of the building where they had been escorted by Miss Warkworth an hour earlier.

They followed the sound of raised voices to find Miss Warkworth hopping from foot to foot outside Monsieur Etienne's cottage.

"He just stormed in," she said, her hand fluttering on her chest. "He looked like a madman. I think he is going to do Monsieur Etienne harm."

Jane eyed the door, starting forward as she heard a crash. With only a momentary hesitation, she rushed inside.

"Captain Robertson, stop!" she shouted, aghast as she realised the captain had Monsieur Etienne by the neck. He was exerting such pressure the French teacher's face was turning red. "Do not do this. You will hang if you kill him."

Her words had no effect and Jane felt a swell of panic as a horrible gurgling noise came from Monsieur Etienne's mouth.

Lunging forward she grabbed hold of Captain Robertson's arm, pulling with all her strength. As she looked up into his eyes, she saw a terrible emptiness there and wondered if she would be able to reach him.

"Do not do this," she said quietly but firmly.

It felt as though time slowed as she saw him fight his instincts, but the relief when he let go of Monsieur Etienne's neck with a cry of frustration was all-consuming.

The French teacher stumbled and gasped, clawing at his neck until Cassandra stepped up and led him to a chair.

"Breathe slowly and deeply," she instructed him, one hand pressed on his shoulder to keep him from rising.

Captain Robertson seemed to deflate, his shoulders sagging and tears streaming down his cheeks. "Look up there," he said, motioning towards the staircase at the back of the room.

"You will not touch him if I go up?"

"No. Not unless he tries to leave."

Jane ascended slowly, hearing every creak and groan of the old wood under her feet. Upstairs there was only one room, the shutters thrown open so it was bathed in sunlight. There was a large bed pushed against one wall and a trunk at the foot. The rest of the space was taken up with artistic materials. Canvases were stacked against one wall, with an easel and paint positioned in front of a chaise longue.

The canvas on the easel was half finished, a painting of a dark-haired young woman walking through the woods. She wore a flimsy dress, almost transparent, and one sleeve had slipped down to reveal a milky white shoulder and breast. The other paintings Jane could see were similar in style. One featured a golden-haired woman reclining on a bed of autumn leaves, almost naked except for a wispy piece of material placed across her hips. Another showed a naked woman walking in an orchard that looked much like the one Monsieur Etienne had taken her and Cassandra to earlier on.

She jumped as Captain Robertson came up the stairs behind her. He pointed at the picture of the golden-haired woman. "That is Lily Tolbeck," he said.

Jane nodded. They knew she had modelled for Monsieur Etienne; he had told them that himself. This wasn't the painting of Juliet on her balcony he had talked about, but it wasn't necessarily suspicious that he had used her likeness in another picture.

"And that is Eliza Drayson." Captain Robertson motioned towards the picture of the naked woman in the orchard and Jane drew in a sharp breath. The man downstairs had denied knowing Eliza, yet here she was in a painting in his bedroom.

"Is there anything of Rebecca here?"

Captain Robertson shook his head. "No, but that doesn't mean he didn't kill her."

Jane looked at the paintings again. They were damning pieces of evidence. They could now prove that Monsieur Etienne knew all three victims.

"We must take him to the magistrate," said Captain Robertson.

Jane inhaled sharply. Mr Margill was corrupt and useless; his involvement would only complicate matters.

"Please, wait a little longer. Let us at least question Monsieur Etienne one more time."

"The time for questioning is over. That man needs to be locked away to safeguard the women of Charmouth and Lyme Regis."

Before Jane could argue further, Captain Robertson disappeared down the stairs. Jane hurried after him, glad to see Monsieur Etienne had regained his normal colour and was now sipping a glass of whisky or something similar. He struggled to his feet as Captain Robertson returned, a look of fear on his face.

"You're coming with me," Captain Robertson said, grabbing him roughly by the arm.

"I am not going anywhere."

"You cannot mean to drag him all the way over the cliffs to Mr Margill's house," Jane said, incredulous. By the grim set of the captain's mouth and the squaring of his shoulders, Jane could see this was exactly his plan. "Surely it is better to send someone to ride for the magistrate and keep Monsieur Etienne here under guard, where there is less chance of escape."

Captain Robertson hesitated and then nodded. "Fine. I will stay with him, though."

"Of course."

"I will go," Cassandra said.

"Go to the inn. There will be a boy there who can ride over to Mr Margill's house." Captain Robertson held out a few coins. "Give him this and tell him to ride fast."

Jane cast around for paper and a pen and after a moment found some, leaning over the small table to write a note for Cassandra to give to the messenger boy to take to the magistrate.

"There. Be careful."

"I will," Cassandra said, squeezing Jane's hand. She leaned in closer and spoke so only Jane could hear. "Ask your questions now. I doubt you will get another chance once Monsieur Etienne is in the magistrate's custody."

Cassandra left, hurrying out of the cottage and disappearing into the gardens. Miss Warkworth was still outside, hovering with indecision, but as Cassandra passed her it jolted her into action.

"This is most irregular, Captain Robertson," she said. "You cannot treat Monsieur Etienne like this. He has done nothing wrong."

Captain Robertson turned to the headmistress. "There are three young women dead, and he has paintings of two of them naked upstairs. Do not talk to me about his innocence."

Miss Warkworth paled and then with a glance at Monsieur Etienne dashed up the stairs to the small bedroom above. She was gone only a minute, but when she came back down her face was ashen and her hands shaking.

Without another word she left the small cottage, and Jane watched as she made her way back to the school building.

Jane took a seat across from Monsieur Etienne. He seemed to have shrunk since they last saw him and sat with his shoulders hunched and one hand still rubbing his neck.

"How do you fare now?" Jane enquired.

"I can barely breathe. This madman has damaged something."

"I am sure the doctor can be called once you are in the custody of the magistrate," Captain Robertson growled.

"I have done nothing wrong," he said, his tone a mixture of pleading and defiance.

"You told us you did not know Eliza Drayson," said Jane. "Yet there is a painting of her upstairs, posing naked in the school orchard."

Monsieur Etienne looked away and didn't answer.

"When Mr Margill arrives, he will arrest you for the murder of Lily Tolbeck, Eliza Drayson and Rebecca Robertson. You will be taken to the county gaol to await trial. I have borne witness to many of these affairs now, and believe me when I tell you the evidence they have here is enough to convict you, after which you will hang."

Monsieur Etienne paled but remained silent.

"Why did you lie about knowing Eliza Drayson?"

Monsieur Etienne gave an almost theatrical sigh. "I was trying to avoid *this*."

Jane waited for him to elaborate and after a moment he continued.

"All right. I knew Eliza and I knew Lily."

"You painted them both?"

"Yes. Eliza modelled for me soon after I first arrived in Charmouth. She needed the money and it is usual for artists to use prostitutes to sit for them — they have less inhibitions." He grimaced and waved a hand. "Eliza was young, much younger than I had initially thought, but there was something captivating about her. She had such a sadness in her eyes. We talked and she told me of her horrible life, the future she saw for herself." He shrugged. "One thing led to another."

"You were intimate?"

"We were."

"Eliza had a child not long before she died. She gave the baby to a childless couple in Sidmouth to raise. Was that child yours?"

He shrugged again. "She seemed to think so, but who can be sure? She told me I was the only one she had been with, but I did not believe her. Her family had to eat, and the only thing she had worth selling was her body."

Jane was taken aback at the callous way he spoke of his previous lover. She wondered what the women who had fallen for his charm would think if they could hear him now. "You carried on seeing Eliza when she was pregnant?"

"Yes, she had this beauty about her. I wanted to capture it for my work."

Jane bit back her contempt. "You made her promises? To take her away from here and start a new life together?"

He shrugged. "In the heat of our passion, I meant them. You have to understand our relationship. Sometimes we would see each other three times a week, sometimes not for a month."

Jane shifted in her chair as she realised this man had likely been the one to promise Eliza a better life, only to snatch those dreams away from her. "But you had no intention of marrying her, of claiming your child, or taking her away from Charmouth?"

"No. I doubt she believed me anyway," Monsieur Etienne said with a flick of his wrist. "Eliza didn't have the privilege of education like the girls here, but she was not stupid. She knew how the world worked."

"She told her friend she had a better life waiting for her," Jane said, unable to keep the disgust from her voice.

Monsieur Etienne looked down, not meeting her eye.

"You never came forward, when she was found dead? You didn't tell anyone of your relationship?"

"What point would that have served?"

"What about Lily Tolbeck?"

He didn't speak for a moment, and Jane saw sorrow in his eyes that hadn't been there a moment earlier.

"Lily was beautiful. You've seen the painting and it doesn't do her beauty justice. I saw her one day down by the harbour and I almost tripped over my own feet I was so astounded by her poise and grace. She was a goddess and did not belong amongst the fishermen and the labourers. That first time I saw her, I knew I had to paint her. I obsessed about her for days, walking to the harbour in the hope of catching a glimpse of her again. Finally she agreed to model for me, and when she did I felt as though my world was whole. She was what had been missing — my inspiration, my muse."

"You were intimate with Lily as well?"

"We could not have helped ourselves, even if the future of the world depended on it."

"What happened to Lily, Monsieur Etienne?"

He gripped the arm of the chair. "I do not know. One evening I waved her goodbye, and the next day she did not meet me when she was supposed to. Later, I heard her body had been found on the beach." He shook his head. "I was devastated. I did not know how I was going to carry on."

"Did you kill her?"

Monsieur Etienne glared at Jane. "How could you even ask such a thing? I loved her. She was the best thing that had ever happened to me."

"Yet after her death you carried on seeing Eliza Drayson."

He shrugged. "Eliza didn't know about Lily, and with my muse gone I needed to keep painting. It was the only thing that dulled the pain."

"And then Eliza died too."

He looked uncomfortable now and Jane realised he was nervous, having had a second lover die only months after the first.

"Yes. I have to admit that worried me, Miss Austen. Both the women I was close to were dead, both found on the beach, but the coroner ruled they were both accidents. I mourned Lily and Eliza and then I moved on."

He didn't seem aware of how callous he sounded, and Jane wondered if he had ever truly cared for Lily or Eliza.

"You can see how damning this all sounds, Monsieur Etienne," Jane said.

"I did not kill Lily or Eliza. I loved them."

"Perhaps they were going to leave you."

"No," he said sharply. "They wouldn't have done that."

"What about Rebecca Robertson?"

Now he shook his head vehemently. "I told you, I am no fool. I do not dally with pupils. I have a good life here; I would not do anything to jeopardise that. Miss Warkworth is a generous mistress, but she would not tolerate a dalliance between a teacher and a pupil. It would ruin the reputation of the school. If I did something like that I would be out on the road."

"Rebecca was not a pupil any longer."

He shrugged. "Still, it was not worth the risk. She was a pretty girl, but she was not one of mine."

"Cad and scoundrel," Captain Robertson growled from his position by the door. "After everything you have said about Miss Tolbeck and Miss Drayson, you expect us to believe you have even the smallest set of morals? You used those poor girls and when you were done with them, you made sure they could never tell anyone about you, leaving you free to prey on Rebecca."

"I did not ever dally with your sister," Monsieur Etienne said again, his voice rising. "I never even sketched her."

"We have the drawings you did of her," Captain Robertson said.

Monsieur Etienne looked up, a flare of anger in his eyes. "They are not mine. Compare them to my work — they will be different. They're not mine, I tell you."

Captain Robertson snorted and Jane felt a wave of exhaustion spread through her. It was difficult to know if he was telling the truth. Monsieur Etienne sounded sincere, but she had thought the same in the orchard, when he had denied even knowing Eliza Drayson.

"You favoured Rebecca, though?" Jane asked. "When she was a pupil here, you chose her above the others to bestow your attention on."

"The young ladies here are so sheltered. They are never allowed to mix with young gentlemen, and so when they encounter a man they are not related to they sometimes lose their sense a little. Rebecca was not like the others; she brushed me off and that was refreshing. If I remember correctly, it was Miss Ringwood who used to stare after me longingly and press little tokens into my fingers." He gave a dismissive wave of his hand. "And the other girl, Miss Wright, she would try to impress me with her French conversation, even though she was not a linguist."

"How about after Rebecca finished here?"

"I saw her half a dozen times in the last year — brief conversations in passing. That was all."

CHAPTER FOURTEEN

Jane was glad when the knock at the door came. "What an interesting little party we have here," Sir Phillip said as he entered the room. Mr Margill followed him in, looking around him with interest. The last man to enter the small cottage was Lord Willingham, who nodded in acknowledgement to Captain Robertson. Jane frowned, wondering why the baron and the coroner were here.

"I hear you have uncovered the murderer, Captain Robertson," Sir Phillip said, taking charge of the situation, despite Mr Margill being the magistrate.

"This man has intimate paintings of Eliza Drayson and Lily Tolbeck upstairs in his bedroom, and he taught Rebecca at Miss Warkworth's school."

"Compelling evidence. Do you deny knowing all three victims, Mr Etienne?"

"I knew them," Monsieur Etienne said, his face turning pale as if he was only just realising the seriousness of the situation. The arrival of three powerful men made him sit a little straighter. "But so did half the town."

"Not intimately," Captain Robertson said.

"I did not know Rebecca intimately."

Captain Robertson scoffed and turned away.

"I will take a look upstairs," Mr Margill said, crouching to avoid hitting his head on a low beam.

"You must be pleased, Miss Austen," Sir Phillip said quietly whilst they awaited the return of the magistrate. "To have identified your culprit so quickly."

Jane did not answer. As on their previous encounters, she felt unsettled by the coroner. He had a superior little smile on his face, as if he knew more than she did, and she half expected him to produce a last-minute alibi for the French teacher.

"Grotesque pictures," Mr Margill said as he descended the stairs. "You clearly corrupted these innocent young women and then killed them. Stand up, Mr Etienne. You need to come with me, and I will arrange transport to the county gaol whilst you await trial."

"I am not a murderer. I loved Lily and I would never hurt Eliza."

"Quiet!" Mr Margill barked, gripping Monsieur Etienne by the shoulder and pulling him to his feet. "Start walking."

Monsieur Etienne looked around in a panic, as if realising this might be the last time he ever set eyes on his home, and then was pushed out the door by Mr Margill.

Sir Phillip and Lord Willingham followed, Jane trailing behind with Captain Robertson last out the door. Outside, Miss Warkworth stood looking flustered, and in the distance a group of schoolgirls huddled together, watching anxiously. As Monsieur Etienne was roughly manhandled away, one of the girls dashed forward.

"Leave him alone!" she shouted, bold enough to reach up and tug on Mr Margill's arm. He thrust her away, sending her scuttling back over the path and into a flower bed. Miss Warkworth was by her side immediately, helping the girl up and soothing her.

Without a word, Mr Margill marched his prisoner through the side gate and out to the road beyond.

Cassandra was waiting outside, watching the proceedings with a concerned expression on her face.

"This has been made into a public spectacle," Cassandra murmured as Jane came and took her arm. She nodded at the group of townspeople from Charmouth, who were gathered a little further down the road. As Monsieur Etienne was pushed up into a waiting carriage, one man bent to pick up a rock, but at a scathing look from Sir Phillip he dropped it and slid away through the crowd.

The carriage trundled off down the road and Jane was left with Cassandra, feeling uneasy about how the events of the day had unfolded.

Captain Robertson approached, his expression grim. "I should escort you back to your rooms."

"Thank you." Jane didn't want to be cooped up in the stuffy rooms at Mrs Riley's, but she knew she needed to honour her promise to her parents to stay safe, even if everyone else was convinced they had their murderer taken into custody.

Jane, Cassandra and Captain Robertson were silent as they climbed the coastal path up the cliff and began the walk back to Lyme Regis. Captain Robertson was walking fast, striding out ahead before seeming to remember his companions and pausing to allow them to catch up before striding off again. After a while Cassandra laid a hand on the captain's arm, halting him.

"You look unwell, Captain."

He shook his head vigorously and then ran a hand across his brow.

"It is not weakness to show emotion," Cassandra said. "Anyone would struggle with everything you have had to endure these last few days."

For a long time Captain Robertson did not answer, then he turned to Jane. "Do you think they have the right man?"

Back at Monsieur Etienne's cottage he had been so certain that the French teacher was the murderer that it was strange to hear him doubt it now. He had a desperate, haunted look in his eyes and for a moment he looked as though he might collapse.

Jane hesitated. She needed time to work through everything in her mind, to go over what Monsieur Etienne had said, to pull it apart and work out what was truth and what was lies, as well as the motivation behind those lies.

"I do not know," she said. "He may be — there is certainly a lot for him to answer to."

"A mountain of evidence," Captain Robertson said.

"Yet..." Jane couldn't help herself, cursing the word even as she spoke it out loud.

"You have doubts, Miss Austen?"

"I have studied the pictures your sister had hidden in her bedroom, and I saw the work Monsieur Etienne produced. Both were made by talented artists, but I am not convinced they are by the same man."

"Surely one man might draw and paint in different styles. How likely is it that there is a second man, someone who was able to get close to Rebecca, who was also a talented artist?"

"That is the thing: the drawings are impressive, and they show a close study of their subject and pretty pencil work, but they are nowhere near the standard of Monsieur Etienne's paintings. It seems possible one was produced by a talented amateur and another by an artist who lives and breathes for his art."

Captain Robertson fell silent, and Jane wished she could rid herself of the nagging doubt. Something didn't feel right, despite the evidence of the paintings and the fact that Monsieur Etienne had so easily lied to her and Cassandra when they had questioned him earlier. He lied easily, the honeyed words slipping from his tongue with no hesitation, and that made him a dangerous man, but it did not necessarily make him a murderer.

"Perhaps he has charmed me like he charmed everyone else," Jane said, hoping it was not the truth. She had always prided herself on being able to see through the superficial to the person beneath, but perhaps this time Monsieur Etienne had deceived her.

"Perhaps," Captain Robertson said and then let out a deep sigh. "I fear I was too eager to grasp onto the idea of a suspect. What if Monsieur Etienne is nothing more than a man with loose morals? I have pushed the magistrate to arrest him and as such stopped looking for other suspects. I may be the reason Rebecca's killer still walks free."

"You cannot think like that," Jane said firmly. "You have done nothing wrong; the guilt should lie only on the shoulders of the man who has murdered Rebecca, no one else. Cassandra and I will not rest on our laurels now Monsieur Etienne has been arrested. We will continue to question and probe, to ferret out the truth, whether that confirms Monsieur Etienne is the man we seek or that we should be looking at another."

"Thank you," Captain Robertson said, clasping Jane's hand. "I am sorry if my actions today made that task harder than it should be."

They walked the rest of the way to Lyme Regis in silence, Jane taking the opportunity to go over in her mind all the evidence against Monsieur Etienne. By the time Captain Robertson bade them farewell, she had more questions than answers.

Arm in arm, Jane and Cassandra knocked on the door to their parents' room and were ushered inside by Mrs Austen, who was holding a letter and looking happier than she had for days.

"This morning I received a letter from Edward," she said before Jane could tell her their news. "He has been given Godmersham Park. Mrs Knight has moved out and suggested he take charge of the estate, and he invites us to go and stay with him for a few weeks."

"That is wonderful news," Cassandra said, taking the letter from her mother's hand. She took a moment to read the note and then smiled broadly. "He says the gardens and parkland are most beautiful this time of year, and he wishes for us to see Godmersham Park in all its glory."

Mrs Austen turned to Jane. "It is important we support your brother, Jane. He is master of an even bigger estate now, and as his family we should visit as soon as possible."

"Of course, Mama," Jane said, taking the letter to read in turn once Cassandra had finished. She felt a thrill of pleasure at the idea of going to stay with Edward and his wife Elizabeth in Kent. Edward had been adopted by the Knights when he was just a boy and as a consequence had split his time between the Knight and the Austen households. It meant that over the years Jane had not spent as much time with him as her other brothers, but she welcomed the idea of spending a few weeks in his new home.

"I will start to pack, and your father will look into organising the journey."

"Mama," Jane said quietly.

"No, Jane. Your brother has issued an invitation and it is important we accept."

"We could accept in a couple of days' time," Jane said softly.

"I want to leave this horrible town. I cannot walk abroad without people whispering and staring, and everywhere I go I worry there is a murderer around the next corner. I haven't slept in two nights for worry about you and Cassandra."

"A man was arrested today," Jane said quickly.

The look of surprise on her mother's face was almost comical. "Arrested? For the murders?"

"Yes, Mama. Monsieur Etienne — he was Rebecca Robertson's French teacher at Miss Warkworth's School for Young Ladies. He knew the other two young women who were killed as well. Mr Margill, the local magistrate, has taken him into custody and transported him to the county gaol."

"Well, that is wonderful news," Mrs Austen said, beaming. "What a relief. That poor girl's family will be able to mourn in peace, and you do not have to worry about this matter any longer." She looked around almost frantically, nodding at everyone in the room. "And there is nothing to stop us from leaving straight away to visit Edward."

"Rebecca's funeral is tomorrow," Jane said, measuring her words carefully. A man may have been arrested, but she was still planning on continuing her investigation. However, she had reached the point where she might have to do that without her parents' consent or knowledge. "I would like to go."

Mrs Austen frowned, but Mr Austen nodded in agreement. "Of course, Jane. It would only be right to show your support to Miss Robertson's family by attending the funeral. I will accompany you and Cassandra, if your mother is too busy with packing."

"Thank you."

"I suppose one extra day will not make too much difference to Edward," Mrs Austen said, unable to stay gloomy for long when faced with the prospect of reuniting with another of her children. "Tomorrow, after the funeral, we will pack our things. With luck, the day after we will secure seats on the coach to Sidmouth, and then we can find the best way to continue our journey."

CHAPTER FIFTEEN

Jane had persuaded her father and Cassandra to set out for the church a whole hour before the funeral was due to begin, to ensure they could slip into a pew and observe people as they arrived to offer their condolences to the Robertson family. Despite their early arrival they were not the first, with a few friends and neighbours of the Robertsons gathering outside. Those who had been closest to Rebecca would no doubt accompany her coffin as it travelled the short distance from the Robertson family home to the church, but many others from the town would come directly here. Rebecca's death had shaken the whole community, and Jane wasn't surprised to see a large number of people begin to assemble.

They took a seat near the back of the church. Their position had an excellent view of the door and allowed Jane to see people as they walked in and took their places. Lyme Regis was not a large place, and even out of the people she had not been introduced to there were not many she had not seen out and about.

"What are you looking for, Jane?" Cassandra asked as Jane shifted in her seat.

"We know Lily and Eliza were both involved with Monsieur Etienne, but he was so adamant that he was not involved with Rebecca I want to see if I can spot anyone else who could have been her mystery gentleman."

"You think Rebecca could have had a separate gentleman admirer?" Cassandra looked puzzled. "Why would Monsieur Etienne kill Rebecca if that was the case? Surely the whole case hinges on one person having a motive to kill all three women."

"I know," Jane said, trying to rein in her frustration. Cassandra was right: it didn't make sense unless the three victims were all connected in some way. "I have been going over this in my head, and I have come up with four possibilities."

Jane glanced around to check no one else was listening and then started listing them on her fingers. "One, Monsieur Etienne is a consummate liar and was romantically involved with Eliza, Lily and Rebecca. He killed them for reasons known only to him. Perhaps because of lovers' quarrels, or because he got bored of them and they stood in the way of future conquests." This idea was the most logical, and Jane could see it was the option Cassandra favoured. "Two, Monsieur Etienne is telling the truth and he was only romantically involved with Eliza and Lily. He killed them in some sort of passionate haze and then somehow Rebecca found out and he killed her to keep her silent."

"But she was going to meet her gentleman on the night she died," Cassandra said, shaking her head. "If she knew what Monsieur Etienne was capable of, I doubt she would have agreed to meet him in the middle of the night on a beach where two other young women had been killed."

"You're right, of course," Jane said. "Strike that theory. Three, as well as their dalliances with Monsieur Etienne, Eliza and Lily were meeting another man — a man who then moved on to Rebecca after they were dead. Or four, it is someone else entirely. Eliza and Lily had their affairs with Monsieur Etienne, Rebecca had hers with her mystery man, and someone else killed the three young women for an unrelated reason."

"Neither of those sound very likely, do they?"

"No," Jane conceded. "I do not hold out much hope for Monsieur Etienne. Yet I still think it important we observe the men here today. If Rebecca's secret gentleman is not Monsieur Etienne, then there is a good chance he will be here amongst the mourners."

"Why are you so reluctant to accept the French teacher as a convincing subject, Jane?" Cassandra asked, lowering her voice even further as an elderly couple came to sit in the pew in front of them.

Jane considered this question carefully, for it was a good one and worthy of some thought. There was a nagging doubt inside her, despite the evidence, something that told her she should not stop searching yet. She had never claimed to be an expert in these sorts of investigations, unlike her mentor, Lord Hinchbrooke. She had only been involved in bringing people to justice for a few years, yet in that time she had slowly learned to trust her instincts.

"I cannot put my finger on the exact reason, but I feel uneasy." She firmly believed that the unconscious mind took in more than the conscious side, and sometimes it was that information, absorbed without acknowledgement, that led to these gut feelings. "It doesn't sit nicely."

They fell silent as Lord Willingham entered the church, and a murmur rippled through the mourners at his arrival. By his side was a younger man, as upright and aloof as the baron.

"That must be one of the sons," Jane said. "Lucy said she saw Mr Thomas Willingham talking with Rebecca on the cliffs not long before Rebecca died."

"You are clutching at phantoms, Jane Austen," Cassandra said, a hint of amusement in her voice. "Lucy also said he told her he was back from university and enquired after the health of her family."

"We have to consider everyone. He is handsome, is he not? In an aloof, severe sort of way."

Cassandra regarded him for a moment and then gave a reluctant nod. "I suppose so, although his manner is not very inviting."

"Much like his father's. Do you find it odd how involved Lord Willingham is in the lives of the Robertsons?"

"Perhaps he feels a sense of responsibility after Mr Robertson died whilst in his employ."

"Yes, I expect he does. He has been most generous to the Robertson family. Providing the money for an education for Rebecca and Francesca, helping Captain Robertson with his commission, supplying the two daughters with dowries and providing the cottage they all live in at a reduced rent."

"Only you could find such generosity suspicious, Jane."

"Perhaps he is simply a generous man," Jane murmured. "But it was strange that he turned up at Monsieur Etienne's cottage with Sir Phillip and Mr Margill yesterday."

Cassandra shrugged. "Is it really that strange? You know full well what men of that class are like. They think everything is their business and expect everyone to accommodate them. It could simply be that Lord Willingham was visiting Mr Margill when the note arrived summoning him to Charmouth, and Lord Willingham thought it would be diverting to accompany them."

"You may be right," Jane said, her eyes still on Lord Willingham and his son. They were dressed sombrely, but their clothes marked them out as a good few social classes above the rest of the people in attendance.

A few minutes later Mrs Mabel Nielson, Eliza Drayson's friend, entered the church, accompanied by her husband. He looked unhappy, and Jane caught a snippet of their conversation as they passed.

"I barely knew the girl. Only to doff my cap to in the street," Mr Nielson was saying, his voice low with a note of petulance.

"I knew her. She would stop and say good morning if I was out with the children. The least we can do is pay our respects today."

"It's macabre, making a funeral into a spectacle like this," Mr Nielson grumbled, and then they moved away to the right-hand side of the church, taking a seat in a half empty pew, out of earshot.

"Mr Nielson isn't happy about being dragged along today," Jane observed. "I wonder how many of these people really knew Rebecca and how many are here to see what gossip they might ferret out."

"You are terrible, Jane," Cassandra said, her hand covering her mouth.

A hush fell over the church as the vicar entered, opening the double doors at the front to signal the coffin was approaching. Everyone stood, the last few mourners from town hurrying in and taking their places before the doorway darkened once again and the coffin was carried in.

Jane felt a lump form in her throat. She thought of the body on the beach, lifeless and abandoned, and then of the girl Rebecca's friends and family had spoken of: a beautiful young woman who had been kind and generous.

Rebecca's immediate family followed the coffin in. Captain Robertson was well turned out in his bright red jacket, light reflecting off the highly polished buttons. Mrs Robertson looked tired, the weight of everyone's eyes making her shrink even further into herself. Francesca had a grim expression on her face and seemed to be doing her very best not to burst into tears.

A few other women walked in beside the Robertson family, all of a similar age to Mrs Robertson, and Jane supposed they were probably her friends or close relatives. These would be the women who would support her over the coming weeks and months as everyone else got on with their lives and slowly forgot about the tragedy that had rocked the Robertson family.

The coffin was placed at the front of the church and the family seated in the first pew as the vicar closed the double doors and slowly made his way down the aisle. As he passed them by, Jane heard him take a shuddering breath. She studied him with renewed interest as he stepped up to the pulpit and laid his hands on the stone surround.

The words of the funeral service were so familiar to Jane she barely had to listen. With her father the rector at Steventon, she had sat quietly whilst he conducted many a funeral for the local people of the village and surrounding countryside.

Instead she watched the vicar, taking in the awkward pause as he gathered his thoughts and the tremor in his voice every time he looked at the coffin. Jane leaned forwards, wishing she had taken a pew closer to the front.

He was a young man, around twenty-five, with short blonde hair and an eager but pleasing face. He was fairly attractive, certainly enough to secure him a wife now he had a sizeable parish and the trappings of the life that went with it.

Jane cocked her head to one side and contemplated him, wondering if this mild-seeming young man could inspire the fervour that prompted Rebecca to keep her beau a secret and made her dream of running away with him.

Often Jane had puzzled over what made two people fall in love. There was physical attraction, of course. There was also the love that came from what one person could do for another. A woman falling for a man of strength to escape an abusive father; a man falling for a woman he knew would provide a happy and comfortable home. Yet most of the time it wasn't just one thing, it was an amalgamation of many tiny characteristics and deeds.

Jane mentally added the vicar to the list of people she wished to talk to, along with the young Mr Willingham.

The congregation bent their heads in prayer and Jane stilled her mind for a moment, dedicating a few minutes to poor Rebecca Robertson.

The rest of the funeral went as expected, with solemn words from the vicar and a silent procession of menfolk to the graveside. The women gathered around Mrs Robertson to escort her home. Outside the church, Jane spotted Lucy Ringwood and Hettie Wright. Both looked pale and drawn and as though they had spent half the morning crying.

"Miss Ringwood, Miss Wright," Jane said as she hurried over, after excusing herself to her father.

"Miss Austen," Miss Wright said, bringing a handkerchief to her eyes. "Such a sad day."

Jane turned to Lucy Ringwood to express her condolences, but the young woman burst into tears and turned her head away, before muttering something unintelligible and hurrying off.

"You must excuse Lucy. It has been a most difficult few days. We heard about Monsieur Etienne's arrest last night. Lucy came running to my house in shock. I think it has shaken her that a man she admired could be responsible for Rebecca's death."

"I think there are a lot of people who feel the same," Jane said, thinking of how Miss Warkworth and the girls at the school had reacted when the French teacher had been arrested. "He is a very charming man."

"Do you think him guilty, Miss Austen?"

Jane hesitated for a moment and saw the flare of interest in Miss Wright's eyes. She may have been the more logical one of Rebecca's friends, but she still didn't wish to believe her old French teacher could be responsible for three deaths.

"I am not sure as yet. There is much to point to him, but nothing I have seen as yet that is irrefutable proof."

"You will keep looking, then?"

"Yes."

"I will tell Lucy as much. Are you returning to the Robertsons' house now?"

Jane looked over her shoulder to where her father and Cassandra stood, knowing that if she returned to their lodgings she would have an afternoon of packing ahead of her. "Yes," she said quickly. "Will I see you there?"

Miss Wright sighed. "It depends on if I can persuade Lucy to come. I do not think she should walk back alone when she is like this. I do not want her to see where Rebecca's body was found without the distraction of a companion to walk with."

"You are a true friend, Miss Wright," Jane said.

Once Miss Wright had left, hurrying after Miss Ringwood, Jane steeled herself for the possible confrontation with her father. She doubted he would argue too much out here in the street, but just gently remind her of the promise she had made to her mother.

"I should go to the Robertsons' house," she said. "Especially if we plan to leave in the next few days. To give the family my best wishes."

Mr Austen stared at her for a moment and then nodded. "Of course."

She let out a surprised little sigh; she hadn't expected it to be that easy to persuade him.

"Cassandra will go with you, and I will go about arranging transport for our journey to see your brother. Say your goodbyes, Jane. I do not think your mother will tolerate any further delay in leaving this place."

"I understand, Father," she said, her heart sinking.

CHAPTER SIXTEEN

"Shall we go to the Robertsons' cottage?" Cassandra suggested as she linked her arm through Jane's. Most of the mourners had dispersed now, with the family and close friends heading through the narrow streets to raise a glass to Rebecca, and other more casual acquaintances wandering off in various directions to return to their homes or their work.

"Let us linger a few more minutes," Jane said, eyeing up the door of the church. The coffin should be in the grave now, and as they looked round the edge of the church they saw the solitary figure of Captain Robertson standing by it. Jane wondered if his family would ever recover from this tragedy, or if it would be the defining event of all their lives. She expected Captain Robertson would mourn his sister but in time, with his life in the army to occupy him, he would be able to move on and fulfil his ambitions. Likewise for Francesca. One day in the not-too-distant future she would find a husband and start a family. It would be Mrs Robertson who was stuck in perpetual grief. First a widow and then a mother who had lost her child in the most horrific way possible.

Jane didn't approach Captain Robertson but instead led Cassandra round to the front of the church and back through the main door. The only person inside was the vicar, who was lighting a candle near the altar, his expression tortured.

He turned as he heard Jane and Cassandra enter and tried to fix his features into a more neutral expression.

"It was a lovely funeral service," Jane said, watching as the vicar's cheeks flushed at the compliment. He was an easy man to read, the type that wore their every emotion on their face, whether they liked it or not.

"Thank you, Miss…?"

"Austen, Miss Jane Austen, and this is my sister, Miss Cassandra Austen. I wonder if you might have a moment to talk?"

The vicar swallowed and indicated a pew. "Please, take a seat."

Jane and Cassandra perched on the wooden bench whilst the vicar took up a place in front of them, turning so he was facing them.

"What can I help you with?"

"From the warm way you spoke of Rebecca, I assume you knew her?"

"Yes. She attended church every Sunday and she was a kind young woman, generous with her time. If ever we needed volunteers to help with church events, she would be one of the first to step forward."

"Everyone has told us how kind she was."

"Her death is a travesty. I am pleased they have arrested that man over in Charmouth."

"Monsieur Etienne, yes. Did you know him?"

The vicar grimaced. "Only by reputation. I understand he was not a godly man."

"If Rebecca often helped out with church events, you must have got to know her quite well," Jane said.

"Naturally, we talked a little."

"I suspect you are an easy man to confide in, Reverend."

"A number of my congregation have told me so."

"I expect Rebecca confided in you?"

The vicar shifted uncomfortably.

"Was it difficult to hear her hopes and dreams with another man when you fostered a desire to be with Miss Robertson yourself?"

The vicar paled and Jane saw she had struck on at least a partial truth.

"I did nothing I shouldn't," he said quickly.

Jane adopted a conspiratorial tone. "Of course not, a moral, upstanding man like yourself would not act on these thoughts." She watched him carefully but saw no sign of deception when he nodded quickly. "Sometimes the Lord sends us something to tempt us, to test us," she said, ignoring the pointed look she received from Cassandra.

"I have been so sinful," the vicar said, head bowed, his voice barely more than a whisper. "The Lord chose to test me and I failed miserably. Miss Robertson wanted nothing more from me than friendship, a listening ear and sometimes a word of guidance, but I admit I was not always a true friend to her. I thought of myself when giving advice, hoping one day she would notice me."

"What did she confide in you?"

The vicar sighed and for a moment Jane thought he might plead the clergyman's right of confidentiality, but after a moment he spoke.

"A few months ago, she told me her conscience was burdened by a secret. I did not press her at the time, but later she returned and told me of a gentleman she was in love with. She said their relationship was difficult; there were people who would not approve. Yet she told me she could not bow to the pressure of society because she loved this man."

"That must have crushed your hopes," Jane said quietly.

"It did. I am afraid I snapped at her a little and told her that if her family were to disapprove, it was for good reason and

171

she should listen to them. She looked taken aback, but before she left she said it was not her family who would disapprove."

Jane frowned. Something pulled at the edge of her consciousness. "She said it was *his* family who would disapprove?"

"She didn't clarify. She just said it wasn't her family."

Exchanging a glance with Cassandra, Jane motioned for him to continue.

"I didn't see her for a few weeks after that, and when I did things were a little strained between us. I apologised for speaking too bluntly and she conceded I was only speaking out of concern. We parted on better terms, but I think she avoided me after that." He looked down at his hands. "As well she might. I expect she realised the regard I held her in and was not keen on me expressing my feelings further."

"Did you express them further?" Jane asked. "Perhaps by sending her a letter or a poem or some other token of your affection?"

"No. I may be a foolish, weak-willed man, but I knew there was little chance for me. I resolved to wait, to see what happened with Miss Robertson and her admirer. If there was a change in circumstance, I would sweep in and declare my feelings then." He shook his head. "I think there is no uglier sin than jealousy, and I succumbed to it so easily. I resolved to dedicate myself to God and studying the Bible, and hopefully if things changed I would be worthy of her."

Jane could see no hint of deception on the vicar's face. He looked crestfallen, totally destroyed.

"You have no idea who this man could be?"

"I thought…" He trailed off, looking at Jane, searching her face. "I thought Monsieur Etienne had been arrested?"

172

"He has." She didn't reveal any more and didn't say anything about the burgeoning doubt inside her.

"Come, Jane. I am sure the reverend would like a few moments to himself." Cassandra stood, smoothing down her skirts and smiling reassuringly at the vicar. "Take comfort in the knowledge you have done nothing wrong, Reverend. We were put on this earth to love one another; please do not berate yourself too much for thinking you had found that in Miss Robertson."

They left the vicar sitting morosely at the front of the church and retreated outside into the warm morning air.

"I think Monsieur Etienne was telling the truth," Jane said, feeling a knot of tension in her stomach as she said the words out loud.

"You do not think he killed anyone?"

"I am unsure about that, but I do not think he was romantically involved with Rebecca Robertson." Jane sighed loudly. "There are too many things in this case that do not fit. Why would Monsieur Etienne deny that relationship when he admitted to the others? Why would Rebecca say it was not her family that would disapprove? They certainly would not want her dallying with a scoundrel like Monsieur Etienne, whereas he doesn't have anyone here in England to warn him off."

"It brings us back to the beginning, Jane. Who was Rebecca going out to meet on the night she was killed? Who was her mystery gentleman?"

"I think we need to go and look at those drawings again. Then I have an idea."

They walked quickly through the town, Jane pulling her bonnet low to protect her face against the sun. It was hot and sunny again today, the cooler weather of the previous days only a momentary reprieve from the high temperatures that had plagued them over the last few weeks. Fortunately, there was a light breeze, bringing a salty taste to Jane's lips — a constant reminder they were at the seaside.

Only a few close friends remained at the Robertson house, and when they approached Francesca slipped out of the front door to greet them. She was dressed in sombre black with her hair in a plait down her back.

"Miss Jane and Miss Cassandra," she said, a fleeting smile on her face. "I was hoping you would visit. My brother tells me Monsieur Etienne has been accused of the murders. Mother is relieved to have an answer."

Jane felt a stab of guilt as she realised what it would do to Mrs Robertson if she burst in and said she thought the magistrate had made a mistake.

Francesca looked at her keenly and tilted her head to one side. "I was surprised."

"That Monsieur Etienne could be the killer?"

The young girl considered this for a moment. "That wasn't what I meant, but yes I suppose I do find that surprising."

"You thought him charming?"

Francesca pulled a face halfway between disgust and amusement. "*He* thought he was charming. The school is only small, and he is the only male in residence, so he has a captive audience, but I was always surprised by how many of the girls became infatuated with him." She gave them a measured look. "And not just the girls. Miss Warkworth too. She would blush and act all coy when he was around, completely out of character. Some of the girls would laugh when she wasn't around."

"It would seem you saw him clearest of all. Yet you still think it surprising he was a murderer?"

Francesca took a moment to consider her answer before speaking, leading Jane and Cassandra into the little garden at the side of the cottage. "Half the girls at school would swoon and forget everything they had ever learned about protecting their virtue if Monsieur Etienne smiled at them. I know he had female visitors from the town as well. I heard Miss Warkworth berate him for it. Anyone else would have been dismissed on the spot, but not Monsieur Etienne." Francesca fiddled with a loose piece of wood on the bench, pulling at it with her nails. "I don't understand why he would kill anyone. Surely if you can charm half the female population with a smile and a few honeyed words, you can get what you want from people without having to resort to violence. Rebecca warned me about Monsieur Etienne, told me what a cad he was. She said she expected an intelligent girl like me to be able to see through his charms, no matter how much he complimented me."

"She didn't find him attractive?"

"I am sure she could see he had beautiful eyes and a nice smile, but no, I didn't think she found him attractive." Francesca let out a sudden laugh. "She told me she used to take walks with him around the gardens when Miss Warkworth was watching, just to rile the old woman up."

"It does not sound like she would start an illicit affair with Monsieur Etienne," Jane said, biting her lip. "Francesca, do you think we could look at the pictures again, the ones that we found hidden in the cushion the other day?"

"Of course. Sam knows where they are. Shall I go and ask him?"

"Yes. Gently, though. I think your brother would like this whole ordeal to be over."

"I will tread carefully."

Francesca disappeared inside the house and Jane sat back on the bench, exhaling softly.

"Rebecca saw through Monsieur Etienne's charm," Jane said quietly. "How likely is it she would have succumbed to it a year later, after warning her sister about the man?"

Cassandra looked thoughtful. "Unless something drastically changed or she got to see him in a different light, I think it unlikely she would go from loathing the man to risking her entire future for him."

"I agree," Jane said.

Francesca returned, the folded papers in her hand, and passed them to Jane. Carefully Jane opened them up, one by one, studying the pictures again. She thought back to the paintings in Monsieur Etienne's bedroom studio, the way he had used the brush strokes, the lightness and elegance of his work. The drawings were equally beautiful, but undeniably different in style. It was not inconceivable that they could have been done by the same person, especially if that person was a talented artist like Monsieur Etienne, but she thought it unlikely.

"Do you think I might borrow these?" Jane asked. "I have a theory I would like to test, and it will be easier if I have the drawings with me."

"Of course."

"How does your mother fare, Francesca?"

"Today has taken a lot out of her. I think she will need to rest once the last of the guests have gone."

"Have you everything you need?"

"Yes, thank you."

Jane wondered if she should tell the young girl she and Cassandra might have to leave Lyme Regis before they could see the case through to a conclusion. If her father managed to deigning to sit, instead standing by the open double doors, frowning at everyone.

Jane felt overwhelmed for a moment. She had to tread carefully if she were to draw out a confession from Thomas with his father present.

She pulled out the pieces of paper Francesca Robertson had given her, smoothing them flat on her lap.

"You are a talented artist, Mr Willingham." She hesitated for a second and then passed the pictures over. "I never met Miss Robertson when she was alive, but even I can see this is an incredible likeness."

Thomas stared at the pictures and Jane wondered if he would deny they were his. His next words, however, confirmed what she had suspected.

"I have always liked to draw, but every picture I produced I was dissatisfied with, until I met Rebecca."

"Tell me how you met Rebecca," Jane said softly.

"I knew Rebecca from childhood, but I hadn't seen her in years," Thomas said, flicking a quick look at Lord Willingham. "When I came home from university, my father kept me busy on the estate, but every so often I would go into town. I met Rebecca once on the road and we stopped to talk. It was a beautiful sunny day and we took a detour through the fields. We ended up spending hours together. That was the start of it." Thomas regarded Jane with a pleading look in his eyes. "You have to understand that what we had was special. Rebecca was like no one I have ever known before. It didn't matter that our lives had been so different, that we had experienced the world in such different ways. All that mattered was being together."

Jane had once thought herself to be in love, a passing infatuation with a man who had decided to eschew their connection in favour of the wishes of his family for him to make a better union. Cassandra had experienced true love. She had loved her fiancé, Thomas Fowle, with a true and steady heart, mourning him deeply when he had died. Their love had been one of equals, with both of them wanting the same things from life — namely a family home and the comfort of each other.

"The Robertsons are good people, but Rebecca would not have been an appropriate wife for my son," Lord Willingham said, his tone cold. Jane thought of the care and attention he had paid the Robertson family, and couldn't marry his actions with his words.

"You knew about their relationship?" Jane asked Lord Willingham.

"I suspected. Thomas had been seen on a couple of occasions leaving the house late at night and although I did not know who he was meeting, I could be fairly confident it wasn't anyone suitable, otherwise the young lady would have been introduced over the dinner table rather than kept secret like a…" He trailed off as his son shot him a contemptuous look. The relationship between father and son was strained, and Jane wondered how much Lord Willingham knew.

Thomas turned to Jane. "Despite knowing what our families would say, or more specifically what *my* family would say, Rebecca and I were going to get married."

Lord Willingham snorted, but Jane pressed on.

"You knew your father would not approve of the relationship, so you started courting Rebecaa in secret. Is that correct, Mr Willingham?"

Thomas nodded.

"When did it start?"

"About four months ago."

Jane kicked at the stone again, making it skitter away over the dark sand. "I also think Mr Willingham knew Eliza Drayson better than he admitted."

"You think he was one of her customers when she was selling her body at her mother's behest?"

"Perhaps. Maybe when he was back from university for the summer months. It is not difficult to imagine him having a few too many drinks and accepting the offer of company from Eliza. He certainly looked guilty when we brought up her name."

"He didn't know Lily, though."

"No," Jane said slowly. "It is a conundrum. Monsieur Etienne is currently our main suspect — he could have killed the two women he was romantically involved with, but there isn't much of a motive for him to kill Rebecca. Then there is Mr Willingham, who could have killed Rebecca and, at a stretch, Eliza, but he wasn't acquainted with Lily."

"Do you think we've had it wrong all this time, Jane? Do you think there is more than one killer?"

Jane didn't answer, the question troubling her. It was difficult to imagine two men in these tiny seaside towns becoming so unsettled in mind that they turned to murder at the same time. It would be quite a coincidence. Another thought occurred to her.

"Lord Willingham is an interesting man, is he not?"

"Interesting?"

"I cannot fathom his motives. He is overly generous to the Robertson family. I know Mr Robertson died whilst working on the Willingham estate, but even so, Lord Willingham has been helping the Robertsons for years. Even a compassionate man might decide a lifelong reduction in rent to be enough, but he buys Captain Robertson a commission and pays the school fees for both Rebecca and Francesca."

"You think perhaps he feels guilty about something?"

"There is nothing like guilt to play on one's conscience. I think something must have happened to Mr Robertson — perhaps his death wasn't completely blameless."

Cassandra puffed out her cheeks and looked out into the distance. "That is quite the accusation to make, especially when you are levelling it at a baron."

"I am not saying he killed the man, far from it, but there are many ways a man can die that are not deliberate but not unavoidable either. Remember Bill Stevens."

Bill Stevens had been employed to clean windows at an estate close to Steventon. He had been up a rickety old ladder with his bucket and cloth when a groom had lost control of the hunting dogs he was bringing into the kennels. The dogs had darted after some small rodent they had spotted, barrelling into the ladder and causing it to crash to the ground. Bill Stevens had fallen, cracked his head and died immediately. It had been an accident, but if he had been provided with a sturdier ladder, or the groom had maintained better control of the dogs, he would still be alive.

"I doubt you will get an answer all these years on. If something did happen, Lord Willingham is hardly going to tell you."

Jane nodded in agreement. It was true. If Lord Willingham was the only one who knew what had happened when Mr Robertson had died, he was hardly going to tell them if it implicated him.

"Another thing that is bothering me is why Mr Margill and Sir Phillip visited Lily Tolbeck's family to assure them her death had been an accident. She was the first to have been

Jane was about to thank Mrs Patterson for her time when the older woman spoke again.

"There was one death, but I am not sure if it is what you are looking for. It happened around the same time as Mr Robertson died, so the details were always a little lost in the upset that followed his death."

Brimming with anticipation, Jane resisted the urge to hurry Mrs Patterson along with the story.

"There was a young girl — I think she was called Mary. She had a job as a servant in Lord Willingham's house. She wasn't from around here, which is why I didn't think of her at first. From what I can remember she was an orphan and started working for Lord Willingham as a maid." Mrs Patterson paused, tapping her fingers on the counter in a bid to help her memory before continuing. "She must have been there for about a year before she died. She was a melancholy little thing, mousy in character. You know the sort. She would scurry through town, not meeting anyone's eye as if there was a great beast snapping at her heels."

Jane nodded, wondering what had brought a young orphan to this part of the world. She supposed a job was a job, and if you had no family tying you to one area, it would perhaps be easier to move somewhere completely new.

"She would come to church every Sunday, but sit at the very back and slip out before anyone could talk to her." Mrs Patterson sighed. "It doesn't make her end any less tragic, though. She took her own life — threw herself down a steep flight of stairs leading to the kitchen at the Willingham house."

"It was definitely a suicide?"

"Apparently the housekeeper found a note in her room when they were packing up Mary's things."

"Do you know how old Mary was when she died?"

"Around sixteen or seventeen, I would think. I know what the Bible says about suicides, but I hope our good Lord has mercy on that poor child. She cannot have known much love or kindness in this world, and I do not like to think of her suffering for eternity in the next."

"I take it she was buried?"

"Yes, though it was all rather overshadowed by poor Mr Robertson's death."

"It happened around the same time as Mr Robertson's death?"

"The same day, I think. Mr Robertson had his accident first, and then whilst everyone was preoccupied, Mary..." Mrs Patterson trailed off.

"Threw herself down the stairs," Jane concluded, then murmured, "I wonder..."

"You cannot think there is a connection between Mary and the deaths that came later?"

Jane forced her lips into a reassuring smile and shook her head. "No, I doubt it. Are there any other deaths you can recall, anything involving a young woman?"

"No, as I say, only the normal spread of the old or infirm succumbing to fevers in the middle of the winter."

"Thank you, Mrs Patterson. You have been most helpful."

Jane and Cassandra took their leave of the shopkeeper and hurried out of the shop. Once outside, Cassandra looked dubiously up at the sky. "I do not think Mama will be happy if we stay out much longer."

"We are so close to uncovering the truth, Cassandra. If we leave tomorrow, then Monsieur Etienne will be hanged for something I am coming to believe he did not do."

"You promised, Jane. You cannot renege on a promise like that."

Grimly Jane looped her arm through Cassandra's as they walked away from the haberdashery. "Let us hope Father was not able to arrange transport for tomorrow, lest I be forced to choose between disappointing my mother and saving a man's life."

CHAPTER NINETEEN

"It has been hours, girls," Mrs Austen said, bustling out to meet them as they came up the stairs. "The funeral finished a long time ago. Where have you been?"

"We went to offer the Robertsons our condolences," Jane said, not liking deceiving her mother. "Then we went for a stroll on the beach."

"At least you got a little fresh air. The sea air really is wonderful, and I am not sure when we will be able to experience it again."

With a sinking feeling in the pit of her stomach, Jane peered over her mother's shoulder, seeing their big trunk open next to the bed.

"Am I to assume father managed to book transport for us?"

"Yes. A carriage to Sidmouth departing the day after tomorrow. It will be easier to arrange our onward journey from there."

Jane exhaled loudly in relief, earning her a curious look from Mrs Austen. Thankfully, her mother was in good spirits now their departure had been confirmed, and she didn't question Jane any further.

"I think I will see if some water can be brought up before dinner. I feel the need to freshen up."

"Mrs Riley had some water brought to your room about twenty minutes ago. It will not be hot any longer, but it should still be warm enough to wash in."

In their room a heavy jug of water sat next to a small basin. Jane touched the jug and was pleased to feel it still retained some heat. She removed her bonnet and smoothed down her hair, longing for a long soak in a bath. They had a small bath at home, one that took an age to fill, but sometimes Jane would persuade her mother or sister to help her bring jug after jug of hot water to the bath placed in front of the fire. Then, when it was filled almost to the brim, she would slip in, lie back and close her eyes, savouring the warmth. At those moments she would envy the Romans and their famed baths, the large complexes she had read about in books where they had whole rooms of heated water to lounge in.

Today she had to make do with a small bowl of tepid water, but even that felt good as she dabbed the washcloth against her skin.

Cassandra had flopped down on the bed after kicking off her shoes.

"Have you worked it out?" Cassandra said suddenly. "You have that look on your face, the one that you get when you puzzle through a particularly difficult problem and come out the other side."

"I think I am almost there," Jane said. "If only I could work out the motive for killing all the women."

"Do you have proof?"

Jane shook her head. Slowly, all the pieces were slotting into place, but much was built on supposition and without proof there was no need for anyone to admit to anything. Sir Phillip and Mr Margill had already shown their ability to ignore the truth, to pick the most convenient solution to suit the narrative they wanted to portray.

"There is no proof. It isn't like the killer conveniently left a slip of paper by the side of each body or a footprint we could match to his own."

"Then Monsieur Etienne will be condemned."

"I know. He is not wealthy or well connected, he is a foreigner and he is an artist. Any one of those things alone would be enough to prejudice a jury against him, but with all of it stacked up he has no chance."

"We only have one day, Jane."

"I know. I think we need to do something bold."

Cassandra pushed herself up onto her elbows. "Bold?"

"Yes. I think I can push Mr Willingham into revealing more if his father is not present."

"What do you propose?"

Jane paused, knowing her plan could be considered underhand, but not sure how else she was going to solve this case in the limited time they had left. "I am going to impersonate Mrs Robertson."

"Jane!" Cassandra's tone was a mixture of shock and admonishment.

"I am going to send Mr Willingham a note, asking him to meet Mrs Robertson, and then I am going to press him without his father present."

Cassandra sighed and flopped back onto the bed. "Tread carefully, Jane. Once we have left Lyme Regis, these people have to pick up the pieces of their shattered lives and start to rebuild."

With a sudden flare of anger, Jane turned to her sister. "I think only of the Robertsons and the Draysons and the Tolbecks. Imagine if we do not uncover the true culprit and in six months' time Francesca Robertson is approached by this as yet unknown man. Imagine if he courts her and flatters her and promises her the world. She would not be suspicious of him because she would think her sister's killer long dead, brought to justice for his crimes."

Cassandra stood and crossed the room, pulling Jane into her arms. "I do not meant to doubt you, Jane. I know your motives are entirely altruistic. There is nothing for you to gain here — everyone is aware of that. This responsibility you have brought onto yourself is weighty, and I wish I could help you more with the burden, but in the end it is always you standing alone against the evil we encounter."

"That is not true. You are my strongest supporter in everything, Cassandra. I would not achieve anything in my life if it were not for your quiet and determined encouragement."

Jane rested her head on her sister's shoulder. They stayed locked together for over a minute before Cassandra stepped away.

"Listen to me very carefully. Do not ever give up on your quest for the truth. No one else is able to unravel this mess, but I believe you can and I will be there by your side every step of the way."

Squaring her shoulders, Jane lifted her chin and straightened her back. "Tomorrow we will get to the bottom of this, once and for all."

They had one more day, no more. If the matter was not settled then, she doubted anyone else would carry on the fight in her absence. Captain Robertson sought the truth, but he had so far been blinded by his hatred for Monsieur Etienne, thinking the teacher had taken advantage of his sister.

Unsurprisingly Jane slept poorly, tossing and turning throughout the night as she tried to imagine the various different ways the men she was going to confront might react. There was a real chance she might be stopped early in the day, silenced by Sir Phillip and Mr Margill. She would have to use all her cunning to ensure she was able to speak freely.

She dressed as soon as the sun was up, sitting at the little writing desk by the window, but today she did not even try to look at her current manuscript. 'Lady Susan' would wait — there was no rush to finish the book. Today all her focus had to be on the accusations she was going to make.

Breakfast was a quiet affair, with Mrs Austen trying to make conversation but everyone else giving short answers. After five minutes, even Mrs Austen sunk into near silence.

"I do not know what you are planning today, girls," Mr Austen said as Jane was about to excuse herself. "But I think I should accompany you."

Jane shot a concerned look at Cassandra. Their father's presence, normally reassuring and welcome, would not be helpful today. Jane was going to have to trick and cajole the truth from people, and she was not sure she wanted her father to see her do that.

"We are ging to visit Mrs Robertson, Captain Robertson and Francesca," Cassandra said.

Mr Austen looked at them with raised eyebrows.

"Your father will accompany you," Mrs Austen said with an air of finality.

"There is no need if you wish to prepare for the journey tomorrow," Jane said, trying to suppress the note of panic in her voice.

"Your mother has everything in hand," Mr Austen said, smiling serenely.

"Two days ago you were present when a scoundrel was arrested for murder," Mrs Austen said, giving both her daughters hard stares. "Yesterday you disappeared for hours after poor Miss Robertson's funeral to somewhere you have not disclosed, and today it is obvious you are planning something."

Jane opened her mouth to protest, but Mrs Austen silenced her with a commanding finger.

"This is not Steventon, Jane. You are not at Lord Hinchbrooke's side and you do not have his protection. Your father and I have been lenient, but this matter is not up for negotiation. Your father will accompany you to wherever it is you are going, or you may spend the day here with me. We can read and do some embroidery."

There was silence as Jane composed herself before turning to her father. "I plan to leave in fifteen minutes if that is agreeable, Father."

"Of course, Jane."

She hurried upstairs, trying not to despair. Cassandra was close behind her.

"What shall we do?"

"We have to continue with the plan. This is our last chance."

Fifteen minutes later Jane and Cassandra waited downstairs for their father to emerge. He ambled down the stairs and beamed at them, taking his hat from a hook on the wall.

"Shall we?" He motioned for Jane and Cassandra to step outside first and then followed them, lifting his hat in greeting to a couple who were walking past.

With a heavy step Jane led the way through the town to the Robertsons' house, hoping they were not too early to pay a call. In polite society, social calls were normally saved until the afternoon, especially when you did not know the person you were visiting all that well. Morning calls were reserved for very good friends.

Even so, Jane did not hesitate when she reached the Robertsons' front door. By the end of the day she doubted she would be welcome in many places in Lyme Regis, after the accusations she was about to level, but she hoped Captain

Robertson, with his sensible approach to most things, might forgive her for the upset she was about to cause.

She raised a hand to knock on the door, but her father reached out and gripped it before she could make a noise. Jane looked around, startled.

"Be still a moment, Jane," he said. "I need to know your intentions are good and selfless before I let you walk in there."

"If there was another way…" Jane began and shook her head. "But there isn't, Father."

"Then go with my blessing, my dear. I will be right outside. All you have to do is call and I will come running."

"Thank you," Jane said, her eyes brimming with tears.

Mr Austen took a seat on the stone wall outside the little house, making himself comfortable, as if he knew he would be there for some time.

Turning back to the door Jane knocked quickly, feeling her heart pound in her chest as she did so.

It took a minute for the door to be opened. A bleary-eyed Mrs Robertson looked out, smiling warmly at Jane and Cassandra when she saw them.

"Come in, come in," she said, ushering them inside. She led them through to the kitchen and pressed them to sit. Francesca was cooking eggs and Jane realised they had caught the family preparing breakfast.

"I am sorry to call so early," Jane said, looking up as Captain Robertson came into the room. He was smartly turned out as usual, his boots clicking on the flagstone floor.

"You are welcome any time, Miss Austen," Mrs Robertson said. "I was horrified to hear of Monsieur Etienne's arrest." The words caught in her throat and she struggled to continue, having to take a few seconds to compose herself before pushing on. "Though I did feel a modicum of relief, knowing the murderer is behind bars."

Jane felt Captain Robertson's eyes on her and glanced up quickly. Her cheeks flushed as his eyes bore into her.

"I have something difficult to tell you," Jane said, drawing out her words as she checked the little clock on the wall over Mrs Robertson's shoulder. It was a little after ten o'clock.

"Difficult?" Mrs Robertson said, looking between Jane and her son. "I don't understand."

"You had better be certain of what you are about to say, Miss Austen," Captain Robertson said, his voice low, a hint of warning in his tone. "I do not want my mother or Francesca to suffer unnecessarily if you are not."

"I am sure, Captain — at least of the first thing I am about to tell you. Two days ago Monsieur Etienne confessed to having an intimate relationship with both Eliza Drayson and Lily Tolbeck. I suspect he is the father of Eliza Drayson's second child. As you know, he is an artist as well as a teacher, and he considered both women to be his muse at one point or another. He promised them both that he would take them away from the drudgery of their lives, to give them a better future."

"Is that what he promised Rebecca too?"

Jane paused, gathering herself before continuing. "In Monsieur Etienne's cottage, there were paintings of Eliza and Lily. Irrefutable proof that he knew them both well. There was nothing of Rebecca."

Mrs Robertson closed her eyes and Captain Robertson shifted uncomfortably.

"What is more, Monsieur Etienne admitted his relationships with Eliza and Lily, but he strongly denied ever being close to Rebecca."

"What are you saying?" Mrs Robertson said.

"Rebecca didn't like him, Mama," Francesca said quietly. She had been sitting motionless ever since serving up the eggs she had been cooking, not touching her own breakfast. Now she rose up, a defiant tone to her voice. "Rebecca couldn't stand him — she warned me about him. She said he tried to play the girls off against one another, make them jealous of whoever he gave more attention to. She disliked him and felt contempt for those of her friends who fell under his spell."

Mrs Robertson looked in confusion from her daughter to Jane. "I do not understand."

"After Monsieur Etienne was arrested, I could not shake the feeling that we were missing something. I spoke to Francesca and she told me that Rebecca was not fooled by Monsieur Etienne's superficial charm."

"You have found the man Rebecca was creeping out at night to see?" Captain Robertson asked, his voice flat.

"Yes."

"Did he kill her?"

Jane swallowed. "I am not sure."

"Who is he?" Mrs Robertson said. Her hands were shaking and she had to clutch them together to try to control them.

"Mr Thomas Willingham."

"No," Mrs Robertson said, shaking her head. "It can't be. Why would Rebecca keep their relationship a secret? We would have been thrilled about a match with the Willinghams. There was no need to hide it."

"No need to keep it secret from *you*," Jane said, trying to be as gentle as possible with the difficult truth. "But Mr Willingham knew his father would never approve of such a match, which is why the courtship proceeded in secret."

"Surely you are not saying Mr Willingham killed Rebecca?" Mrs Robertson was almost in tears now and had two spots of colour deepening on her cheeks.

Jane remained silent. She didn't have a confession, didn't have any proof beyond the relationship Mr Willingham had admitted to. It made him the most likely person to have strangled Rebecca, but there was nothing definitive that a clever man could not argue his way out of in court.

"He came to the funeral yesterday," Captain Robertson said, starting to pace about the room. "He walked up to me and shook my hand and offered his condolences. There wasn't a hint of grief on his face, no remorse or sadness." He stopped suddenly and looked at Jane. "Lord Willingham, does he know?"

"Yes."

Francesca came forward and pressed her mother into a chair, a comforting hand on her shoulder as the older woman broke down into terrible sobs.

Without another word, Captain Robertson stalked from the kitchen, moving through the house at great speed. He flung the door open so hard it crashed against the wall, making the whole house shake.

"Samuel!" Mrs Robertson shouted, looking up in panic. "Samuel, don't do anything rash." She struggled to her feet and before anyone could stop her ran after her son. For a moment Francesca just looked at Jane and Cassandra in amazement, and then she followed her mother and brother.

"Is the timing right?" Cassandra asked, looking at the clock with concern.

"I hope so." Anxiously Jane and Cassandra followed the Robertsons out of the house and past their bemused father, who stood to follow them. They stood no chance of catching

Captain Robertson up, but Jane felt a wave of relief as she saw the Robertsons had stopped only a few hundred yards down the road.

Before they had left their lodgings that morning Jane had arranged for a note to be taken to the Willingham estate to be delivered into Lord Willingham's hands. She had expressed her plan to inform Mrs Robertson of Rebecca's relationship with Mr Willingham and outline her suspicions of his involvement in Rebecca's death. As Jane had hoped, the letter had spurred Lord Willingham and his son into action. They would be aware that they could not stop Jane and Cassandra from breaking the news, but they could control the narrative if they got to the Robertsons first. The story of a heartbroken young man in love, mourning his precious secret fiancé was very different to the one Jane had presented of Mr Willingham forcing Rebecca to keep their relationship secret and then perhaps murdering her.

As Jane had hoped, the commotion as Captain Robertson met Lord Willingham and his son attracted a crowd almost instantly. People began peering out of the houses on either side of the street as well as sidling in from further away to see what was occurring. By the time Jane and Cassandra got to the Robertsons, there were a dozen people there, the number growing all the time.

This was what Jane had wanted. Lord Willingham held all the power in this affair. He was a wealthy, influential man who was friends with all the right people. One whisper in Sir Phillip or Mr Margill's ear and the network of gentlemen closed ranks, protecting their own. It was an almost impenetrable defence, and over the centuries it had meant that if a common man committed a crime he would hang for it, but if a titled man committed the same crime he would almost always get away with it.

Jane had spent the night puzzling over how to break through this line of defence Lord Willingham had placed around his son and had realised the only way to do it was with public opinion. People feared and respected the local landowners. Many were employed by them, rented their properties from them; many aspects of their lives were dependent on the will and whim of Lord Willingham. Individually it was hard to stand up to someone who had the power to destroy you and your family. Yet if you gathered enough people and whipped them up into a frenzy of indignation, the tide could quickly turn. People were empowered by having their neighbours stand beside them. Jane hoped that having the whole town clamouring for answers would mean the Willinghams would be forced to confront them, and she was more likely to get justice for Rebecca. If the choice was between being lynched by an angry mob or the magistrate actually stepping up and arresting Mr Willingham, she hoped Mr Willingham would end up in custody.

"Mrs Robertson," Lord Willingham said from his position high on his horse. "Perhaps we could go somewhere more private to discuss this matter."

"Get down, you coward!" Captain Robertson shouted at Mr Willingham, reaching out and grabbing the young man's leg.

"Get off me!" Mr Willingham shouted, kicking out. His horse side-stepped nervously and for a moment looked like it would rear and throw its rider to the ground.

"You will answer for what you've done!" Captain Robertson shouted, lunging forward again. A murmur ran through the crowd at Captain Robertson's words and Jane saw Lord Willingham regard the assembled people uneasily. He was an astute man. He would know discussing these delicate matters in public would not be good for either him or his son.

"What did he do?" a particularly bold woman called from the crowd.

"Did he kill Rebecca?" another asked, buoyed by the first woman.

"I thought it was that foreigner from the school in Charmouth?"

"The French can't be trusted."

"He looks guilty, up there on that horse."

"He's got a handsome face, the sort of face you should never trust."

The voices were coming thick and fast from the crowd now, and Jane felt a glimmer of hope that her plan might actually work.

"Enough!" Lord Willingham shouted, fixing the assembled crowd with a furious glare. "This is slander, and the next person who says something to bring my son's name into disrepute will face the full consequences in a court of law."

The crowd fell into an uneasy silence and for a moment Jane thought it had all been for nothing, but then Mrs Robertson spoke.

"You knew, didn't you? You knew your son was meeting my daughter."

"We will not discuss this in the street," Lord Willingham said sharply. "I have always been a friend to your family, Mrs Robertson. Do me the courtesy of allowing us some privacy to discuss these delicate matters."

"Get down and face me like a man, Thomas. Stop hiding behind your father!" Captain Robertson's voice broke through. He was completely focussed on Mr Willingham, who was looking flustered. He lacked his father's poise and composure.

Captain Robertson managed to unbalance the younger man, pulling him down from the horse and causing Mr Willingham to land in the dust of the street. Someone darted forward and took hold of the horse's reins, leading the agitated animal from the two men so it could not inflict any damage. The captain hauled Mr Willingham to his feet, holding him by the lapels of his jacket.

"Deny it," Captain Robertson said, his voice low and dangerous. Jane hoped he did not lash out. She would feel responsible for any punishment he received for striking Mr Willingham, but she was aware events were now out of her control. She had set up this confrontation, but she could not influence how things went now. She only hoped the answers they would get would be worth it.

"I loved her," Mr Willingham said.

"Be quiet, foolish boy," his father snapped at him.

"You loved her?"

"I loved her with all my heart. I wanted to marry her, to take her on the adventure she dreamed about. We planned to travel the world together, to see the sights of Greece and Italy and dozens of countries in between."

"Empty promises," Captain Robertson said, still holding Mr Willingham by his jacket. He gave him a little shake. "You were never going to marry her. You thought she was not good enough for marriage." He gave the young man a look of disgust, moving his face closer in a threatening manner. "Rebecca was worth a hundred of you."

"I know," Mr Willingham said and Jane thought she saw tears in his eyes.

With her heart pounding, Jane stepped forward so she was standing next to Captain Robertson. "You loved Rebecca," she said. Her voice was soft, a contrast to the threatening tone of

Captain Robertson, but she made sure it was loud enough for the crowd to hear.

"Yes, I loved her," Mr Willingham said.

"You took long walks over the cliffs with her and met her on the beach long after she should have been in bed."

Mr Willingham nodded, the tears brimming over and falling onto his cheeks.

"You promised her you would be married, despite the objections of your father."

"We would have found a way. We wanted nothing more than to be together."

Jane carried on in the same reasonable tone, aware that any second Lord Willingham might pull her back and whisk his son off to safety. She needed to strike now, needed to confirm what she suspected. Only a confession would do.

"What did Rebecca say when she realised you had killed her father?"

Mr Willingham went pale and shook his head.

"Stop it!" Lord Willingham roared.

"She must have been devastated to find the man she thought she loved, the man she had risked her whole future for, was responsible for the death of her father."

"Do not say a word," Lord Willingham said, directing the command at his son.

"Did she push you away? Did she say she no longer wanted to see you?"

"No."

"Is that why you killed her?"

"No! I didn't kill her. I couldn't hurt her. I loved her."

All around them the crowd was quiet, listening to every word. Captain Robertson was staring in horror at Mr Willingham and somewhere over Jane's shoulder she heard the heavy, laboured breathing of Mrs Robertson as she tried to take everything in.

"I swear I didn't hurt her. I couldn't hurt her," Mr Willingham said, his eyes pleading now. "She didn't know…"

Jane felt a surge of triumph and tried not to let it show on her face. "She didn't know? You never let slip you were responsible for her father's death?"

As Mr Willingham shook his head, Lord Willingham launched himself forward, pushing past Jane and making her stumble. She thought she would fall to the ground, but a strong arm caught her and steadied her. She looked up to find her father by her side.

"Enough!" Mr Austen shouted with an air of authority many didn't know he possessed. He was a mild-mannered man, generous in spirit and always willing to spare his time for his parishioners, yet he was no mere country vicar. He was well educated and astute and able to construct an argument for a debate that few could break. He spoke now in the voice he used when he delivered a sermon. It was commanding and almost impossible to ignore. "There will be no more fisticuffs in the street. We are all reasonable, civilised people and we will conduct ourselves in a suitable manner."

Everyone paused and Jane felt a rush of gratitude towards her father. She was aware he may never let her leave the house again after the scene she had incited this morning, but at least he had got everyone to stop for a moment.

"I suggest we take this matter inside," Mr Austen said. Jane did not protest. The crowd, the frenzy of the mob mentality had done what it had needed to. She had her confession. Now there would be the more delicate job of unpicking the individual strands until there was only the truth left.

CHAPTER TWENTY

It was cramped inside the Robertsons' house with so many people inside. Mrs Robertson sat with Francesca by her side. On the other side of the room Lord Willingham sat stiffly beside his son. Jane, Cassandra and their father were positioned between the two parties, whilst Captain Robertson stood by the door.

After everyone was settled, Mrs Robertson looked at Thomas Willingham.

"You killed my husband?"

There was complete silence in the room for a few seconds before Lord Willingham spoke. "My son did nothing to your husband. Mr Robertson died in a tragic accident."

"He confessed," Captain Robertson said from his position guarding the door. "We have witnesses."

"You have nothing," Lord Willingham spat. "A few people who may or may not have seen a nod of a head. You would be laughed out of court."

Jane leaned forward, seeing she would need to take control or the situation would descend into chaos. "Perhaps I can take you all through the version of events I have settled on from my investigations over the last few days." She stood and took a position where she could see everyone in the room clearly. "I think it is important to lay everything out; only that way will we be able to find our way through to a satisfactory conclusion."

"I didn't kill Rebecca," Thomas said, his eyes wild as they darted around the room.

Jane held up a hand. "We will come to Rebecca in due course," she said. "Please stay calm. We have a lot to cover."

"You said he killed my husband," Mrs Robertson said.

Jane nodded. "Yes, I think that is a good place to start." She looked around the room, checking everyone was attentive before she started. "Perhaps I do not have as trusting and kind a nature as some people, but from the very start I thought it odd that Lord Willingham would be so generous to the Robertson family. Yes, Mr Robertson worked for him on his estate, and he died there, after an accident in the stables, but most employers would salve their conscience with a monetary donation to the man's widow or something similar. Instead the baron continued to support Mr Robertson's family, helping with their rent, with a commission for Captain Robertson, and with school fees for the girls."

"You condemn me for being too generous?" Lord Willingham asked.

"The generosity sparked my curiosity," Jane said. "It made me suspicious, although at first I wasn't even sure what I was suspicious of. Your support of the Robertson family started long before anything happened to Rebecca, so I knew it could not be related to her death. That left Mr Robertson's untimely demise.

"From the start I was troubled by Sir Phillip's and Mr Margill's desire to have the three deaths reported as accidents. At first I thought this was only for Rebecca's death. I could understand their desire to avoid causing any unnecessary panic. It is not pleasant to think there is a killer roaming the streets of Lyme Regis, and I could understand even if I did not agree with their plan to investigate the crime without sending the whole town into uproar." Jane paused, looking over the assembled group. All eyes were on her; all were listening intently. "As the other deaths came to light, it was apparent Sir Phillip and Mr Margill were aware there was someone in the local area strangling young women. Their desire to prevent panic became more understandable, if less palatable. A man capable of killing three people was certainly capable of killing more.

"Then Mrs Tolbeck came forward, the grandmother of the first victim, Lily Tolbeck. She told us that Sir Phillip and Mr Margill had told the family Lily's death was an accident. They hurried through the inquest. These were the same actions we saw after Rebecca's death. Yet at this point there was no pattern — Eliza's murder wasn't until months later, and Rebecca's weeks after that. At the time of Lily's death, there was only one — hers. It made me wonder whether Lily's really was in fact the first death, and that led me to the story of Mary."

At the mention of Mary's name, Thomas Willingham looked up sharply. Lord Willingham held up a hand, warning his son not to say a word.

"Mary was a young orphan, employed as a maid in Lord Willingham's household. From what I can gather, she was a quiet girl who kept to herself. Tragically she died almost six years ago, on the same day Mr Robertson died."

"Mary took her own life," Lord Willingham said sharply.

Jane regarded the older man for a moment and then turned her attention to Thomas. "Shall I tell you what I think happened, Mr Willingham? All you have to do is nod or shake your head."

He looked up at her and then nodded.

"I think you liked Mary. She was quiet and sweet and a similar age to yourself. I suspect you made some advances which she ignored, but one day you came across her alone. I imagine she tried to fight you off, but you wanted her and as the son of her master you felt like you had the right to have her." Jane regarded the young man carefully and saw the flush of shame on his cheeks. "She screamed and you didn't expect that, so you put your hands round her neck and you squeezed, out of anger, out of a desire to shut her up."

Mr Willingham covered his eyes with his hands, and Jane wondered if it was remorse for what he had done or horror at being found out that shamed him.

"My son did not kill anyone," Lord Willingham said curtly, although the exhaustion on his face showed he was a broken man.

"He strangled Mary, and I think Mr Robertson saw him do it. Did you turn on him next?"

Thomas shook his head, unable to speak.

"I will tell you," Lord Willingham said. "Just leave my boy alone." He took a deep breath. "Thomas was, as you say, being a little too physical with Mary. I believe he had his hands around her neck when Mr Robertson happened upon them. He pulled Thomas off the maid and she ran off towards the house. She was alive," he said pointedly. "I do not know if in her distress she tripped at the top of the kitchen stairs or if she threw herself down them."

Mr Willingham let out a low moan, but his father silenced him with a glare.

"Later you placed a note in her room, outlining how unhappy she was, to make it look like a suicide," Jane said.

"I did not want anyone looking too closely. The local doctor was happy enough to overlook the bruising on her neck when it was obvious she had fallen down the stairs, and the note made a verdict of suicide easy to come by."

"What about my husband?" Mrs Robertson said. She had been sitting quietly all through Jane's explanation and now she looked ashen.

"I chased him," Thomas said, startling everyone as he spoke for the first time. "I was livid and I focussed my anger on him. I chased him into the stables and I grabbed him by his shirt and I shook him."

Lord Willingham lowered his head and closed his eyes, as if he knew now nothing would ever be the same again.

"I shook him and I shouted and then I pushed him away from me. I turned around, thinking I would go and find Mary and explain, but then I heard a thud and this terrible silence afterwards." He stopped for a second, looking down at his hands. "I turned back and Mr Robertson was just lying there on the floor, not moving, blood pooling around his head. When I had pushed him he'd stumbled and tripped over a rut in the floor. Then he'd fallen straight back, hitting his head on the stable door. He was dead instantly."

Thomas raised his eyes just enough to glance quickly at Mrs Robertson, but here was no apology, no acknowledgement of the impact his actions had made on the Robertsons' lives.

Jane broke the silence. "Your father cleaned up your mess. He sent you back to school and then university, ensured Mary's death was recorded as a suicide and even tried to pay reparation to the family of a good man who had been killed because he had done the right thing. Then he waited nervously."

Thomas looked up at this and then over at his father. Lord Willingham shifted in his chair but did not say anything.

"He waited nervously, always with an ear to the ground, wondering if that would be the end of it, or if he would hear of some poor young woman raped or strangled. I expect he paid someone to keep watch on you whilst you were at university, Mr Willingham, and then when you returned home he took over the job himself."

"Father?" Thomas said.

"That is why Sir Phillip and Mr Margill were so quick to react when Lily Tolbeck and Eliza Drayson were found dead on the beach. You have influence with these men, and it would have been easy for you to persuade them to push through a narrative of accidental death. I expect you increased your watch on your son, unable to outright accuse him but terrified he might kill again."

"You suspected me?" Mr Willingham said.

Still Lord Willingham didn't answer his son.

"When you found out about Rebecca Robertson and your son, you must have been horrified. What sort of man could even think of courting the daughter of a man he had killed?"

"It wasn't like that," Thomas said. "Mr Robertson's death was an accident. With time, I thought Rebecca might understand and perhaps be able to forgive me."

"Did you tell her?"

"No. I was going to, I just never found the right moment."

Mrs Robertson stood, turning her eyes on Thomas. "I will only ask you this once, and if you ever cared for my daughter you will answer honestly. Did you kill Rebecca?"

"No," Thomas said quickly. "I couldn't harm her. I loved her."

"You strangled that poor maid," Captain Robertson said with disgust.

"I was young … stupid…"

"Youth is no excuse. Even a boy of twelve knows not to place his hands on another to cause harm."

Lord Willingham stood, pulling his son to his feet beside him. "That is enough. We have told you everything."

217

"Not quite everything," Jane said quietly. "I think you knew Miss Eliza Drayson as well, did you not?"

"Yes," Thomas said quietly. "But I have not seen her recently. I didn't kill her, and I knew nothing of the other girl who died."

"I am going to take my son home now," Lord Willingham said firmly. "I am sorry, Mrs Robertson. You have been badly deceived, but I did not think the truth would serve any purpose except ruining my son's life."

"He killed my husband," Mrs Robertson said.

"That was an accident."

Lord Willingham grasped his son by the arm and led him from the room, pushing past Captain Robertson.

"Is there any point in sending for the magistrate?" Captain Robertson asked as he watched the baron and his son hurry up the street. Some of the townspeople were still outside their houses and it must have made for an uncomfortable few minutes for the two men.

"I doubt it," Jane said, feeling a little dejected. "What proof do we have?"

"He murdered my husband," Mrs Robertson said, and Jane was pleased to see Cassandra pull a chair up next to the distraught woman to comfort her.

"He will deny it. Once Lord Willingham has his son under control, they will tell a story of a consensual if over-eager liaison with the maid, and an accidental trip causing your father to fall. If Mr Willingham was born into a different social class, perhaps there would be some hope of justice, but you are not going to get this complaint past the local magistrate." Jane tried to speak as gently as she could, knowing her words would be devastating for Mrs Robertson and her children.

"What about Rebecca?" Captain Robertson said grimly.

Jane pressed her lips together and considered for a moment. "I am not convinced Mr Willingham killed Rebecca," she said. Despite everything he had admitted to, Jane did not think he was the murderer they had been seeking.

"Surely he has to be responsible," Francesca said, her eyes brimming with tears. It was the first time she had spoken since they had all gathered at the house and everyone had taken their seats. "He planned to meet her on the beach, he warned her to keep their relationship secret, and he has a history of losing his temper with women if they do not give him what he wants. He even knew Eliza Drayson."

Jane could see how desperately the family wanted this to be over. It had got to the point where they did not care who the culprit was, as long as the killer was identified and taken into custody by the magistrate.

"I know it is difficult," she said, looking at each person in turn. "But we are almost there. We have uncovered so much already. We do not want to rush this now; it is important to get it right."

"My Jane will see this through," Mr Austen said, and Jane's head whipped round. She had almost forgotten her father was there. "Have faith in her. She will find the killer."

"I think we all need a little rest," Cassandra said, taking Jane's hand. "Perhaps we can gather our thoughts and call on you this afternoon."

"Of course," Captain Robertson said, unable to hide his look of disappointment. Mrs Robertson gave a weak smile and then collapsed into Francesca's embrace.

Outside the air was warm but fresh, and Jane took a few deep breaths.

"You were fantastic, Jane. The way you manipulated Mr Willingham into a confession in the street and then hit him with everything you knew once we were inside. It was masterful."

Jane glanced at her father nervously. He had never seen this side of her before and she worried he would refuse to let her continue her investigation now he had seen how perilous it could be.

"It was quite something to watch," Mr Austen said, reaching out and taking Jane's hand in his own. "I am in awe of how your mind works, how it jumps from one comment or observation to another, connecting them into a picture that no one else can see until you point it all out. You have a rare talent, Jane."

"I worried that you might not approve of how I went about things today."

"I understand that sometimes a little provocation is needed to get people to confess to what they have done. I cannot say I am overjoyed by the danger you could have been in, but I am impressed by how you handled everything."

Impulsively Jane reached out and embraced her father, wrapping her arms around his slender frame. "Thank you. That means more to me than you could know."

"We will not tell your mother the details of today's events, though," Mr Austen said with a smile.

"No, I think that wise."

"Jane, do you know who killed these girls?" Cassandra asked as they walked down the street. "Do you have an idea?"

"I do, but I cannot tell if it is preposterous or not."

"You know?"

"Not for certain, but something has been rattling around in my head ever since we spoke to the vicar after Rebecca's funeral."

"You suspect him?"

"No, but he spoke of jealousy. He was talking about himself, but that doesn't mean we cannot apply it to others too. He said there was no uglier sin than jealousy."

CHAPTER TWENTY-ONE

Jane felt a knot in the pit of her stomach as she approached Sea View House. She was glad of her sister by her side and her father's presence a little behind her. Despite her trepidation, she fixed a determined look on her face before knocking at the door. She disliked the magistrate and the coroner, but she needed them and she refused to be cowed by them.

"Miss Austen to see Mr Margill and Sir Phillip," she said to the footman who opened the door.

Sir Phillip sauntered out of the drawing room, looking like he was master of the house despite it being Mr Margill's residence.

"Ah, Miss Austen, I wondered if you would turn up again. Come in, don't stand on the doorstep."

They entered the house, following Sir Phillip into the drawing room where Mr Margill was seated. He didn't rise as they came in, instead giving them a curt nod.

"What do you want, Miss Austen? The Frenchman is being held in gaol in Dorchester. Surely there is nothing more we need discuss," Mr Margill said.

There was no invitation to sit, so Jane looked around her and chose a comfortable sofa to perch on, eliciting a small chuckle from Sir Phillip.

"We have spent an enlightening morning with the Robertsons and the Willinghams," Jane said. This piqued the interest of both men, as she had thought it would. By the glance they shared, Jane suspected Sir Phillip and Mr Margill were aware of Thomas's past crimes. "I am curious about how much you knew," Jane continued. "I suspect quite a lot. Did you know that a few years ago Mr Thomas Willingham tried to force himself on a household servant, a girl named Mary, before attempting to strangle her? I expect Lord Willingham must have told you when he explained why he wanted Lily Tolbeck's death hushed up. It must have worried you when Eliza Drayson turned up dead as well, then Rebecca Robertson. How many more victims would it have taken before you put the safety of the women of Charmouth and Lyme Regis before the old loyalties and allegiances?"

Mr Margill opened his mouth to answer but Sir Phillip got there first.

"I am sure we have no idea what you are talking about, Miss Austen."

"I am sure you don't," Jane murmured. She sighed. "I am not here to try to place blame, but I do need your help. I think you hold an innocent man in the cells. I do not think Monsieur Etienne is the murderer."

Sir Phillip scoffed. "We are hardly going to release the man based on your gut feeling. For all we know, you might be enamoured of the scoundrel's charm like all these other young women."

"I spoke to him for a very short time only, always in the presence of others. I think he is innocent, Sir Phillip, which means the murderer is still at large. One day, perhaps in six months, perhaps in twelve, they will strike again and then you will have a hard time explaining how people are still being murdered when you hanged the supposed killer months before."

"I suppose you are suggesting Mr Margill arrests Mr Willingham."

"No," Jane said quickly. "Although I do think he has crimes to answer for, I do not think he is the killer of Lily Tolbeck, Eliza Drayson or Rebecca Robertson."

This made Sir Phillip pause and Jane could see his interest was piqued.

"You are not accusing Mr Willingham?"

"No."

"Then who do you suspect?"

Jane took a deep breath before she answered, aware the two men might laugh her from the room.

"I don't know."

Sir Phillip regarded her for a minute. "Correct me if I have not understood, Miss Austen, but you want us to release Monsieur Etienne because you *think* he is not guilty, but you do not have another viable suspect."

"I want you to release Monsieur Etienne," Jane said, holding the coroner's eye, "because I think we can provoke a reaction from the real killer."

This caught his attention, and even Mr Margill sat a little straighter in his chair.

Mr Margill held up a finger and went to the corner of the room. He pulled the bell cord to summon a footman, asking for tea to be brought in. They all waited in silence as the minutes ticked past until the door opened again and a maid entered with a tray of tea and biscuits.

"Leave us, close the door and make sure no one disturbs us," Mr Margill said, raising his voice so the footmen outside could hear. "If I catch anyone listening at the door, they will be out on the streets without their last week of pay."

The maid scurried out, closing the door firmly behind her.

"Well, Miss Austen," Sir Phillip said, picking up a steaming cup of tea. "Tell me your idea."

"Ever since Monsieur Etienne protested that he had never had an intimate relationship with Rebecca Robertson, I have been trying to work out what motive one person might have for killing all three women. At the start of the investigation I assumed all three women were involved with the same man, that something in the relationships had gone wrong and this man had developed a taste for killing."

"Yet Monsieur Etienne tells us he was not intimate with Rebecca Robertson," Sir Phillip said, nodding slowly.

"Mr Willingham was courting Rebecca and had quite possibly paid for Eliza's company in the past, but he did not know Lily."

Sir Phillip raised an eyebrow and motioned for Jane to continue.

"I could not work out why Monsieur Etienne would kill Rebecca, or why Mr Willingham would kill Lily, and then I wondered if my first assumption had been the wrong one."

"You think they were not killed by the same person?" Mr Margill said.

Jane quickly shook her head. "I think it would be highly unlikely two killers would choose the same method, down to luring their victims to the beach to kill them. No, I assumed the young women were killed by the man they were all keeping secret."

"You do not think so now?"

"No. I think the motive was not quite what I had thought."

Sir Phillip took a sip of his tea and Jane could see his mind was flicking through the possibilities, trying to get to the answer.

"There was a common theme when I spoke to Francesca Robertson and some of Rebecca Robertson's friends. They all said how some of the girls vied for attention from Monsieur Etienne. He would favour one girl over the others for a period of time, taking her aside for private conversations and encouraging her in her work."

"I cannot see how this helps to identify the killer," Mr Margill said, but Sir Phillip was nodding slowly now.

"What do we know all the victims had in common?" he murmured.

"Perhaps spell it out for those of us not keeping up," Mr Margill said in irritated tones.

"Of course," Jane said, leaning forward and taking a cup of tea from the tray on the table. "The one thing all three women had in common was that they were having a secret relationship."

"How does that help?" Mr Margill said, sitting back and crossing his arms over his chest.

"Imagine this," Jane said, taking another sip of tea and then placing her cup down on the table. "A woman completely besotted with Monsieur Etienne. She is obsessed with him and reads all the signs he gives her as special — only for her. She builds up a fantasy of them being together, then sees Lily going into his cottage. She is livid, but as can happen with this sort of obsession, she blames Lily rather than Monsieur Etienne. When an opportunity arises to talk to Lily alone, she takes it, but is overcome by rage when Lily will not listen. She strangles her." Jane looked around the room and could see the magistrate and the coroner were at the very least taking time to consider her theory. "Time moves on. Monsieur Etienne mourns Lily, but not all that long, and rekindles his affair with Eliza Drayson, promising her the world in order to get her to come and pose for him so he might paint. History repeats itself: the killer sees another woman entering Monsieur Etienne's cottage and once again lures her to a secret meeting on the beach where she kills her."

"All very plausible," Sir Phillip said. "One of the girls from the school becomes obsessed with Monsieur Etienne, telling herself she had a future with the man despite him never looking at her more than any of the others. She watches who comes and goes into the room of the man she loves. But there are two small problems." He held up two fingers to check them off. "One, to strangle someone requires a good amount of strength. I cannot see a student at the school being able to overpower and kill all three adult women. Two, Miss Robertson did not go into Monsieur Etienne's rooms. If we are to believe Rebecca Robertson did not have an affair with Monsieur Etienne, why would this suspect kill her?"

"To address your first point, I think you are wrong. When provoked, a woman can be very strong indeed. If she was able to take her victims by surprise, she could well have had enough strength to strangle them."

"Perhaps," Sir Phillip said.

"As for your second point, I think we have to assume the killer is not in possession of a stable mind. Before Rebecca's death, she had already killed twice to keep the man she loved for herself. It would not be too much of a stretch to imagine she saw or heard something that she misconstrued as a budding relationship between Rebecca and Monsieur Etienne."

Sir Phillip considered for a minute and then nodded. "Your theory has merit, Miss Austen. Who is it you suspect?"

"I think there are two likely suspects," she said slowly. "Lucy Ringwood, who was a schoolfriend of Miss Robertson's, and Miss Warkworth herself."

"The headmistress?"

"Yes."

"Why do you suspect these two?"

"Lucy Ringwood was quick to come to Monsieur Etienne's defence when her friend spoke poorly of him. She tried to direct our suspicions onto other men when we were talking about who Rebecca's mystery gentleman could be. Miss Warkworth seems stern with the girls in her care but overly lenient when it comes to the actions of Monsieur Etienne."

"Yes," Sir Phillip said. "I did notice her outside the Frenchman's cottage when he was arrested. You have a plan to bring the culprit into the light?"

"A little trickery, yes. If you will transport Monsieur Etienne back to Charmouth and release him, making a show of apologising for the wrongful arrest, we will ask him to come in on the deception. He will announce loudly and repeatedly that he plans to leave Charmouth for good. Then we wait and see who turns up at his door."

"You think the murderer will?"

"If I am right, this woman has loved him from afar for a long time. She will have built up a story in her mind of how they will live happily ever after and will not allow anything to stop that. I think she will declare her love for Monsieur Etienne and ask him to take her with him."

"I cannot see things ending well when he refuses," Sir Phillip said.

"No. We must be prepared for all eventualities."

Sir Phillip considered for a moment and then gave Jane an assessing look. "What if you are wrong, Miss Austen?"

"Then you take Monsieur Etienne back into custody and nothing is lost."

"Except we have told everyone he is innocent. That may hurt the case against him."

"I doubt it. You can spread the rumour that you were trying to see if he had an accomplice, that it was a clever ruse, nothing more."

"That would work," Sir Phillip said and Jane could see he was warming to her idea. She didn't know if it was out of a desire to find the real killer or because he liked the idea of the chaos that would ensue if they released Monsieur Etienne. It didn't really matter as long as he agreed. "What do you think, Margill?"

"I think it is an absurd idea. We have our man locked up in gaol."

"Absurd, yes, but I like it. Let's do it. You'd better ride over personally, Margill. I doubt the guards will arrange for Monsieur Etienne to be transported back to Charmouth without your presence there to confirm things."

"I doubt I will be able to organise it today."

"Nonsense. Take your carriage and you can bring him back in that. It will be a bit slower than on horseback, but at least you will get him here by nightfall."

Margill grumbled as he stood, but moved to obey Sir Phillip's orders. In the hierarchy of society Sir Phillip was the superior, although Mr Margill in his role of magistrate should have the final say when it came to matters of crime and justice.

Sir Phillip turned to Jane. "It will take him some time to get Monsieur Etienne released from gaol and back to Charmouth. I suggest we meet outside Miss Warkworth's school at five o'clock, Miss Austen. Come alone. There will not be room for your entire family to attend you."

Jane had half expected to be shut out of this last stage in the hunt so was pleasantly surprised that Sir Phillip was allowing her to be present. She glanced at her father, wondering if he would object.

"You will be responsible for the safety and welfare of my daughter?" Mr Austen asked.

Sir Phillip waved a dismissive hand. "I doubt there will be any danger, but yes, I will protect her if the need arises."

As Jane stood to take her leave, she felt the familiar surge of excitement course through her body. This evening they would finally get to the truth.

CHAPTER TWENTY-TWO

It was a little after five in the afternoon and Jane was already growing impatient. She was hidden in the upstairs room of Monsieur Etienne's cottage, perched on the stool he must have used when he was painting. There were no comfortable chairs in the room, and she did not want to lounge on the chaise longue he used for his models or even perch on the foot of the bed.

Sir Phillip had directed her upstairs a few minutes earlier after she had sneaked into the school grounds whilst Miss Warkworth was occupied elsewhere. It was important the headmistress did not know Jane was there. If she were the killer, then she had to believe Monsieur Etienne was alone once he had been released by Mr Margill.

To occupy herself she studied the paintings, looking at the vibrant, youthful face of Lily Tolbeck and the haunted beauty of Eliza Drayson. Monsieur Etienne was accomplished; he had captured their essence in the paintings. She only wished the picture of Lily was something more appropriate, which could be given to her grandmother to remember the young woman by.

Outside there was a commotion and Jane watched as Monsieur Etienne strode through the side gate from the street into the gardens of the school, making his way to the cottage. Miss Warkworth was with him as well as half a dozen schoolgirls, all chattering excitedly. Lucy Ringwood wasn't present, but Jane hoped there would be enough gossip for every word Monsieur Etienne uttered to get back to the young woman.

"Thank you for your support," Monsieur Etienne cried, kissing Miss Warkworth's hand and beaming at the students. He seemed to relish his role in this deception and Jane almost believed him as he spoke. "My time in gaol was terrible, worse than you could ever imagine, but I am pleased to have been released and my name cleared in connection with these awful crimes. I will mourn Miss Tolbeck, Miss Drayson and Miss Robertson. Alas, I do not feel I can stay here in Charmouth any longer. I plan to pack up my things and leave in the next few days. I am sorry to be so abrupt in my departure, Miss Warkworth, but I cannot live my life under such a cloud."

Miss Warkworth looked aghast and murmured something Jane could not hear from her position tucked away behind the curtains of the upstairs window.

"I am sorry, madame, but no. I will not reconsider. Tomorrow or at the latest the day after I will leave Charmouth. Perhaps it is time for me to return to France."

He was very convincing, just the right balance of stubborn determination and sadness. Jane watched as he held up a hand, stalling any more questions.

"I am filthy and exhausted. You will have to excuse me. I need to wash and I need to rest."

Without another word he entered the house, closing the door behind him. For a long moment there was no movement downstairs and Jane imagined Monsieur Etienne resting his head against the door. During his short stay in gaol, he had likely imagined he would never see his little cottage again. It was hard to remain positive when the justice system was stacked against you.

Jane heard the creak of floorboards and then Monsieur Etienne appeared at the top of the stairs. He put his finger to his lips and Jane nodded. Miss Warkworth had gone, but a few of the girls still lingered outside the cottage.

"I understand I have you to thank for this little reprieve, Miss Austen," Monsieur Etienne said quietly.

"It was my idea, yes."

"I hope it works. Mr Margill was clear that if no other suspect is identified, I will be taken back to gaol and I will not leave until I go to my trial."

"I hope it works too," Jane said sincerely.

"You suspect Miss Warkworth or Miss Ringwood?"

"Yes."

He nodded thoughtfully. "Miss Warkworth watches me at night, I know that. Sometimes if I have a candle lit and have not yet pulled my curtains, I catch her peeking out at me from her window."

"And Miss Ringwood?"

Monsieur Etienne grimaced. "She follows me if she spots me in town. Hurries to catch up with me. I thought it endearing, a continuation of her schoolgirl infatuation…" He shuddered.

"Sir Phillip has positioned himself nearby, so all we have to do is wait."

"And pray one of those women is responsible so I do not have to go back to that awful gaol."

Jane pressed her lips together and smiled tightly. She could understand his horror at the thought of returning to gaol to await trial. With a guilty verdict all but guaranteed, he would likely be dead within the month. Still, he seemed not to care that if Miss Warkworth or Miss Ringwood were the murderer, they would suffer the same fate.

"I wish to bathe," he said, eyeing Jane up and down. "But I suppose that can wait."

"You are most thoughtful, Monsieur Etienne."

He had just turned to walk down the stairs when there was a knock on the door. He stiffened for a second and then Jane saw his features settle into a serene expression as if he had slipped a mask on.

Jane positioned herself close to the window as she had agreed with Sir Phillip. He was hidden in the grounds with a contingent of men from Mr Margill's household, ready to rush in at Jane's signal. They had agreed only Jane would stay in the house, as the floorboards upstairs were very creaky and Jane was the lightest amongst them. One creak when their suspect came to pay Monsieur Etienne a visit and they might realise it was a trap. Jane would listen in on their conversation and once she had overheard enough, she would signal to the men hidden in the grounds.

Jane did not dare to move as Monsieur Etienne disappeared downstairs. She felt her heart thud in her chest as he opened the door.

"Miss Warkworth," he announced, a little too loudly for it to be natural. Jane hoped he did not give away her presence before any wrongdoing could be confirmed.

"May I come in, Monsieur Etienne? I know it is a little unusual, but I fear if we talk on your doorstep there will be a dozen young ears listening to our conversation. The girls may be pretending to take an interest in the garden, but in truth they are all far too inquisitive for their own good."

"Of course, Miss Warkworth."

There was a momentary pause as Miss Warkworth entered the cottage and closed the door behind her. She was risking her reputation, entering a man's residence without a chaperon like this, and Jane wondered what else she would do to spend time with the French teacher.

"I came to ask you to reconsider," Miss Warkworth said. Her tone was clipped and formal, but there was a hint of underlying emotion.

"Reconsider?"

"Your decision to leave. Please do not act rashly. You are a great teacher, and you will be missed dearly if you leave." She took a deep breath, audible even upstairs. "I will miss you if you leave."

Jane held her breath, wondering if this was the start of the declaration she had hoped for.

"I am sorry," Monsieur Etienne said. "As much as I have loved working here, and working with you, I do not feel I can continue."

There was a long silence before Miss Warkworth spoke again. "Very well. I wish you all the best, Monsieur Etienne. Please do not hesitate to give my name as a reference if you decide to teach again."

With that, there was some shuffling of feet and Miss Warkworth left. Jane felt a crashing disappointment. She had been completely invested in her theory, convinced that after the drama of Monsieur Etienne's release from gaol and declaration that he would be leaving Charmouth, the woman who had killed to keep him to herself would reveal herself.

Monsieur Etienne waited a few minutes then came up the stairs, giving a little shrug as he caught Jane's eye.

"Not Miss Warkworth, I think," he said. "I am glad — she has always been good to me." He grimaced and then sat down on the edge of the bed, looking exhausted. "Although I would rather her neck was stretched on the gallows than my own." He laughed at Jane's horrified expression. "Now we must hope it is one of the other young women you say are infatuated with me."

"Did you see Miss Lucy Ringwood much?"

He shrugged again. "Here and there. She left the school a year ago — since then I might see her a few times a week. The town is small; there are not many places to go."

"Did you feel she held you in a particularly high regard?"

Monsieur Etienne smiled, some of his old confidence returning. "Most ladies hold me in high regard. I think it is my accent, or perhaps my devilish good looks."

A thought occurred to Jane that made her shudder suddenly. "Did it bother you if someone did not succumb to your charm?"

"Like Miss Robertson, you mean?" His expression was serious for a moment before he looked away. "Not at all, Miss Austen. I will admit one grows accustomed to the attention, to the flattery. It can feel strange not to receive it, but thankfully for me it does not happen often. If someone does not wish to spend time with me, it does not affect me at all." He smirked at her. "I focus my attention on those who do wish to be with me."

The sound of chattering from the girls outside drifted up through the window, and Jane wondered if any of these girls would be bold enough to approach the house. She hoped not. It would be disastrous if the students scared away someone planning to visit Monsieur Etienne.

"Perhaps I should be planning to run," Monsieur Etienne said quietly, making Jane's head whip round. He held up his hand. "I do not mean it as an admission of guilt, but you know they will condemn me if there is no other suspect brought forward."

Jane contemplated telling him about Thomas Willingham but decided against it. It would not change anything. Mr Willingham might have been secretly courting Rebecca, but he would never be arrested unless there was indisputable evidence.

"If I made it to France, then I would be able to live my life without looking over my shoulder. My countrymen would not hand me over to your authorities."

Before Jane could answer, there was a knock at the door.

Monsieur Etienne jumped to his feet and hurried downstairs, giving Jane a meaningful look. She quickly got into position so she could be seen by Sir Phillip and his men through the window if she needed to give the signal.

"Monsieur Etienne," a soft voice called as the door opened. Jane strained to hear, and she felt a thrill of anticipation as she realised the voice belonged to Lucy Ringwood. "Jacques." She sounded breathless as she used his first name.

There was the sound of the door closing and then a rustling of clothes.

"Miss Ringwood," Monsieur Etienne exclaimed. "What are you doing?"

"Forgive me, Jacques, but I thought I had lost you."

"Please sit down, Miss Ringwood."

"Lucy. You called me Lucy once."

"A slip of the tongue."

"Don't say that."

"Why are you here, Miss Ringwood?"

"I heard you had been released. I came here as soon as I could. It was awful thinking of you in that filthy gaol, all alone and suffering."

"It was not a pleasant experience."

"You are free now, free to continue with your life."

"Yes, I am thankful."

"I heard you plan to leave Charmouth. I do not blame you, of course. How could you continue to live here when people have been so cruel in their judgement? I think you're right to leave Charmouth, the school, and Miss Warkworth too. She is too controlling. I think she sees you as hers to keep."

"I will leave as soon as I have made arrangements for my journey," Monsieur Etienne said, and Jane had to admire how calm he sounded. He was not pushing her to declare her guilt, which might make her suspicious. Instead he was allowing her to talk as much as she wanted in the hope she might give something damning away.

"Where will you go?"

"To Portsmouth, I think. From there it will be easy to arrange a passage to France."

There was a long silence and Jane had to resist the urge to shift impatiently.

"You cannot leave me behind, Jacques," Miss Ringwood said with a desperate intensity to her voice. "Take me with you."

"Miss Ringwood…"

"I cannot bear to stay in Charmouth any longer. It is stifling. Everything is so dull, every day so mundane. Take me to France with you. It will be such an adventure."

"I cannot just take you to France," Monsieur Etienne said.

"You must."

"What about your father, your friends?"

"What about them? You must know they mean nothing to me when compared to you."

"Miss Ringwood…"

"Lucy," she corrected him, a hint of impatience in her voice now.

"It would be improper for you to come with me."

"What do you care for the rules of society? I love you, Jacques, and I know you love me. We are perfect for one another and now we can finally be together. No more distractions. No more silly girls getting in the way."

"What do you mean?"

"I don't blame you, Jacques. I know you are a passionate man and that men have needs. Lily and Eliza and Rebecca were a way to satisfy those needs."

"Rebecca?"

"You do not have to pretend, Jacques. I said I forgive you."

"You think I had a relationship with Rebecca?"

"I saw you with her, on the cliffs one day. It was obvious by the way you touched her arm."

"What was obvious?"

"That you were intimate. I could see it in her eyes, too. She was always so superior, always talking about starting a new life away from here. She used to laugh at how all the girls would talk of you, and then there she was, seducing you."

"You didn't like the thought of that?"

Jane was impressed by how calmly Monsieur Etienne asked the question. He didn't deny the relationship with Rebecca, instead using it to provoke a reaction. He was completely focussed on his role in eliciting a confession from Lucy.

"No, I didn't like to think of anyone with you, but least of all her. Rebecca always had everything handed to her. Everyone loved her."

"I thought she was your friend?"

"If she was my friend, then she wouldn't have seduced you."

There was a short pause before Monsieur Etienne spoke again.

"What happened with Rebecca, Lucy?"

"You mourn her, even now?"

"No," Monsieur Etienne said quickly. "I just want there to be no secrets between us. Not if we are going to start a new life together."

"You will take me to France with you, Jacques?"

"Of course." He sounded genuine, like a man in love, and Jane marvelled at his skill in the art of deception. "But I need to know what happened."

"You will not be angry?"

"No, I promise."

"Rebecca told me you were going to run away together. I knew she was probably forcing you to go, but I could not risk it."

"She told you that?"

"She didn't use your name, of course. She was always so careful, but I knew. She said that you were just working out the details."

Jane felt a rush of sadness for Rebecca Robertson. She had been planning a new life with Mr Willingham, but her friend's obsession with their former French teacher had meant she would never get to experience anything new ever again.

"She told me once that you met on the beach, that she would sneak out late at night and you would walk along to meet her when the tide was out."

Monsieur Etienne stayed quiet. Jane knew she should signal to Sir Phillip, but she wanted to hear all of Lucy Ringwood's confession.

"I went out several nights, walking along the cliffs, but I never saw you. Then one night there she was on the beach, on her own."

"You went down there?"

"Yes. She was so surprised to see me that it was easy to knock her to the ground, and once she was down I climbed on top of her and put my hands around her neck and squeezed." Lucy paused. "I did it for you, my love, for us."

With a wave of her hand Jane signalled to Sir Phillip from the window, watching as the four young men from Mr Margill's household came running through the garden, followed by Sir Phillip and Mr Margill at a slightly slower pace. They did not knock, instead bursting into the cottage, eliciting a shriek from Lucy.

Jane hurried to the stairs, descending into the chaos.

Lucy Ringwood fought the two men who sought to restrain her, but at the appearance of Sir Phillip and Mr Margill she stilled.

"What is this?" she said, looking desperately at Monsieur Etienne.

"You killed Rebecca, and you killed Lily and Eliza."

Tears welled in Lucy's eyes. "For you, Jacques," she whispered. "I did it all for you."

"No," Monsieur Etienne snapped. "You did it for yourself." He stepped closer to her. "I would never have chosen you."

Lucy let out a wail that seemed to come from somewhere deep inside.

"You would have let me hang for your crimes," Monsieur Etienne said when she quietened.

"No! They wouldn't have hanged you. You weren't guilty — they would have seen that at your trial."

Monsieur Etienne turned abruptly and disappeared up the stairs.

"Jacques!" Lucy shouted, desperation in her voice. "Please, Jacques, come back. Don't abandon me now."

"Enough, Miss Ringwood," Mr Margill said, motioning for his young assistants to take Lucy away.

"I heard her confession," Jane said when it was just Sir Phillip and Mr Margill left. "She admitted to killing Rebecca. I think she might be insane."

"That does not mean she cannot hang for her crimes," Mr Margill said. "She is lucid enough to stand trial."

"Good work, Miss Austen," Sir Phillip said. "Finally, we can put this matter behind us."

Jane was surprised by Sir Phillip's words of congratulations, and it must have shown on her face.

"I am not completely heartless, Miss Austen. I am happy I will not be called to witness another young woman slaughtered on the beach." He nodded in satisfaction and then clapped Mr Margill on the shoulder. "Come, Margill. Let us transport Miss Ringwood to gaol. I wish to be present when she is thrown into a cell."

The two men left and Jane sank down onto one of the chairs next to the table.

"Thank you, Miss Austen," Monsieur Etienne said quietly from behind her. She had not heard him descend the stairs. "If it was not for your persistence, I would still be in gaol. I owe you my life."

"I am pleased your name is cleared. Do you still plan to leave?"

"Yes, I think it is time I returned home. I have a hankering to see my family. I do not know what the future holds, but for now I think I want to surround myself with people who truly love me."

"I wish you the best of luck, Monsieur Etienne," Jane said, standing wearily. She walked out of the cottage into the evening sunlight, ignoring the curious stares of the schoolgirls. As she made her way out of the school grounds, she felt a weight lifting off her shoulders. Finally the case was solved, all the questions answered. Lucy Ringwood would pay for her crimes. Mr Willingham was less likely to face any justice for his actions that had led to the death of Mr Robertson and the young maid Mary years earlier, but she knew that was a battle she would not win.

Slowly Jane walked through the town of Charmouth, breathing in the fresh sea air. For the final time she climbed the cliffs, taking the coastal path towards Lyme Regis. As she reached the spot where she had first seen Rebecca's body a few days earlier, she paused.

"Rest in peace, Rebecca," she murmured.

Now there was nothing on the beach to show the violence that had happened there less than a week before. The sand and the rocks looked as they always did, the sea lapping at an empty shore. For a generation, perhaps two, Rebecca would be remembered, but it saddened Jane to think that after that the young woman's story would be forgotten.

With one last look at the beach she turned and continued along the coastal path, heading back to her family. She was eager to leave Lyme Regis now, to start the journey that would take her, Cassandra and her parents to visit her beloved brother, Edward. There, in the tranquil Kentish countryside, surrounded by those she loved, she would be able to put the ordeal of the last few days behind her.

Whilst she walked Jane thought about the investigation, examining it from every angle to ensure there were no unresolved issues. Jane could not see any. She had identified the two gentlemen the three women were having secret liaisons with. Lucy Ringwood had confessed to Rebecca Robertson's murder, with hopefully a full confession regarding the murders of Lily Tolbeck and Eliza Drayson to follow. She had even uncovered the mystery of what had happened to Mr Robertson on the day he died six years earlier. All in all, it had been a successful, if exhausting, few days.

As she descended from the clifftops, Jane saw a familiar figure waiting at the bottom for her and immediately her spirits felt lighter. Jane ran the last few steps, throwing herself into Cassandra's arms.

"Is it finished?" Cassandra asked.

"It is finished."

EPILOGUE

Four months later

Captain Robertson raised a hand in greeting, hurrying through the crowds to meet Jane and Cassandra. He was dressed in his military uniform, the red jacket vibrant in the sea of darker coloured clothes on the promenade.

"Miss Jane and Miss Cassandra Austen, it is a pleasure to see you again."

"You look well, Captain Robertson," Jane said as they fell into step beside him.

It was the truth. When the Austen family had departed Lyme Regis in the summer, Captain Robertson had been a wreck of a man. Now his demeanour was confident and he looked healthy.

They walked on a little further, weaving through the crowds. It was busy in Southampton and not the easiest place to talk, but it had been a convenient location for this little meeting. Captain Robertson's regiment were stationed nearby for a few weeks, and Jane and Cassandra had a distant cousin who lived on the outskirts of the town and had invited them to visit. Jane had been touched by Captain Robertson's suggestion they meet. She would have understood if the Robertsons never wanted to see her or Cassandra again. They had barrelled into the Robertsons' lives at the worst time, and the family must have associated them with the terrible memories of the death of Rebecca. Yet Captain Robertson had written a few times since they had parted in Lyme Regis and seemed to want their friendship to continue.

Only Mrs Robertson was quiet, and Jane suspected she had slipped into a melancholy these last few months.

"That is what a week of leave will do for a man."

"You have been home?"

"Yes, I got back to my regiment just two days ago."

"How do your mother and Francesca fare?" Cassandra asked.

"Francesca is well. She is settling in at her new boarding school. My mother is understandably struggling, but I think she is a little brighter week by week."

"Does Francesca like her new school?"

"Yes, although I do not think she enjoys being away from home. She worries about Mother. They both send you their warmest regards. Francesca was quite indignant I would not bring her to meet you today, but it is better she stays in school whilst she is settling in."

"I will write," Jane said. Over the past few months she had exchanged half a dozen letters with the young girl, enjoying her tales of her new school friends and the teachers that exasperated them.

"She will like that," Captain Robertson said. His smile faded and his expression turned serious for a moment. "Did you read about the execution?"

Lucy Ringwood had been found guilty of the murder of Lily Tolbeck, Eliza Drayson and Rebecca Robertson a month earlier. She had been hanged for her crimes in a public execution, but the Robertsons had decided not to attend.

"I did. There was a small segment about it in the newspaper our father buys. It said the execution itself was uneventful."

"I am told she confessed to all three murders and that she was repentant during her trial. I wondered if they would hang her, or if they would send her to one of the asylums, but it seems there was no question of her being spared the noose."

"I think she had lost her mind," Jane said quietly. She thought back to the first time she had met Lucy Ringwood, seemingly mourning her friend's death and eager to help catch the culprit. She'd been in possession of her wits enough to be a convincing liar. Yet the woman who had thrown herself at Monsieur Etienne when he was released from gaol had been delusional. She hadn't even realised it was a bad idea to confess her crimes to the man who had been having an affair with two of her victims.

"Mr Margill came to see me, after Miss Ringwood had been found guilty," Captain Robertson said. "He was surprised none of our family had attended the trial. He told me Miss Ringwood went into much detail about the crimes. It sounds like she began to lose her grip on her sanity after her mother died. That was when she started to watch Monsieur Etienne and develop these delusions they would be together. When she saw Eliza Drayson and later Lily Tolbeck sneaking into his cottage, she was distraught. She lured both of them to the beach, making them think they were meeting Monsieur Etienne for a romantic midnight tryst. No doubt they were surprised to see her but not suspicious, and that meant she could get close enough to knock them down and strangle them."

"She must have had quite some strength," Jane murmured.

Captain Robertson let out a deep sigh. "I thought I would feel better," he said. "Once she was dead and the matter put to rest, I thought I would feel some relief, but I don't."

"Because her execution didn't really change anything. Rebecca is still dead and buried, and the death of her murderer is not going to change that," Jane said as she laid a hand on Captain Robertson's arm. "You must not rush yourself to move on. Most wounds heal with time, but it is only four months since you lost Rebecca."

"You are right, of course, Miss Austen. I should not be so impatient."

"I wanted to tell you what happened with Lord Willingham," Captain Robertson said as they paused at a bench overlooking the sea.

Jane looked up with interest. She was convinced Thomas Willingham would never be brought to justice for his role in the death of Captain Robertson's father. Lord Willingham was too wealthy, too well connected.

"Lord Willingham has rented out his house in Lyme Regis and taken his son to Yorkshire to stay with some distant relatives. He paid my mother a visit before he left and assured her that he would dedicate his life to ensuring his son was never a danger to anyone else. I understand Mr Willingham still mourns Rebecca."

"At least your mother will not have to worry about seeing either of them in the town now they have moved far away."

"For that I am grateful. Lord Willingham also settled a substantial amount of money on my mother. She refused to accept it at first; she said nothing could compensate for the loss of my father, but I pressed her to accept."

"It will make her life easier, and Francesca's."

"That is what I told her. There is no need to forgive or forget what Mr Willingham did, and I am certain my father would have urged my mother to take the money. He was a practical man."

"Hopefully that is the last any of you will ever hear from the Willinghams."

Captain Robertson inclined his head. For a moment they were silent. It was a tragic set of circumstances that bound them together, and Jane knew it must be cathartic for Captain Robertson to speak so freely about the events of the last few months. She was sure he would not talk to his fellow officers about the tragedy that had befallen him, not wanting them to look at him any differently.

"I thought I might write to your mother soon," Jane said. She felt deeply for the woman who had lost her husband and her daughter to two different killers. "I wanted to extend an invitation for her to come visit us in Steventon, whenever she feels up to it."

Captain Robertson's face lit up and he nodded eagerly. "I am sure she will be delighted to receive such an invitation. Her mood is understandably low at the moment, but she talks of you with great affection, Miss Austen."

Jane smiled. "Then I will write."

They spoke then of the mundane, of the weather and of family until the sun began to dip. Captain Robertson stood and he bowed first to Cassandra and then to Jane.

"I do not know where my regiment is to be posted next, but I do promise to write. I thank you for your friendship as well as everything you have done for my family."

"I hope circumstance allows us to see you again soon, Captain Robertson. We wish you the best of luck for the next few months."

With a final bow he walked away, leaving Jane and Cassandra sitting on the bench looking out to sea.

"Perhaps we can have a more relaxing time on our next holiday," Cassandra said with a gentle smile. "No more murders."

"Perhaps," Jane said, linking her arm through Cassandra's. "Although maybe just a minor robbery or two. We wouldn't want life to be too dull."

A NOTE TO THE READER

Dear Reader,

Thank you for taking the time to read *The Body on the Beach*. If you enjoyed the book, I have a small favour to ask — please pop across to **Amazon** and **Goodreads** and post a review. I also love to connect with readers through my **Facebook** page, on **Twitter**, **Instagram** and through my **website**. I would love to hear from you.

Laura Martin

Sapere Books is an exciting new publisher of brilliant fiction and popular history.

To find out more about our latest releases and our monthly bargain books visit our website: **saperebooks.com**

Printed in Great Britain
by Amazon